Scooping Up Scandal

Scooping Up Scandal

Little Dog Diner Series

Emmie Lyn

TULE
PUBLISHING

Scooping Up Scandal
Copyright© 2024 Emmie Lyn
Tule Publishing First Printing, August 2024

The Tule Publishing, Inc.

ALL RIGHTS RESERVED

First Publication by Tule Publishing 2024

Cover Designer: Lou Harper, Cover Affairs

No part of this book may be used or reproduced in any manner whatsoever without written permission except in the case of brief quotations embodied in critical articles and reviews.

This is a work of fiction. Names, characters, places, and incidents are products of the author's imagination or are used fictitiously. Any resemblance to actual events, locales, organizations, or persons, living or dead, is entirely coincidental.

AI was not used to create any part of this book and no part of this book may be used for generative training.

ISBN: 978-1-964703-22-0

Chapter One

MY DAY OFF wasn't supposed to start with a phone call startling me half to death. But it did.

I fumbled on the nightstand to silence my ringing phone even before my sleep-deprived brain surfaced through the fog.

"Hello?" I mumbled. The time blinked 5:30 on my watch. Really? Who was making calls at that hour? If I'd been fully awake, I would have checked the caller ID. But you know how it is. I reacted before thinking when caught by surprise. Or when aroused from a deep sleep. Oh, well. Too late to hang up and go back to dreamland. Because an unintelligible whisper came through the phone. Creepy.

Awake now and heart pounding from the unknown, I scooched up against the headboard until I was sitting up straight. Was this a crank call before the sun was barely above Maine's Blueberry Bay? So much for sleeping in on the one day my Little Dog Diner was closed.

Pip, my Jack Russell terrier, looked at me with her head cocked as if asking what was going on? I had no more of a clue than she did.

I heard my name coming through the phone. "Dani? Dani Mackenzie?" The caller seemed confused as if she wasn't sure she had the right number.

At first, I didn't recognize the voice.

"Uh-huh?" I said, wishing I'd let it go to voicemail.

With my husband Luke out of town for a few days, I knew this wasn't his deep, rumbling tone, so I was ready to hang up when I realized he wasn't calling with some kind of emergency.

But then I heard, "It's Cam. Camilla Carter?" Finally, a name to go with the mystery caller. "The *Blueberry Bay Grapevine*? I hope I didn't wake you," she said low.

Why the whisper, I wondered. Was she afraid she'd wake the rest of the neighborhood?

Just then, Pip pushed her head under my arm and knocked the phone loose. When I grabbed it, I hit the speaker button, absently scratching under her ear. Of course, Pip leaned in for more love from me, at the same time Cam's breathing startled me, amplified now and suddenly sounding like a buzzsaw.

"I'm awake," I said, hearing the annoyance in my voice.

"I'm really sorry, Dani." Cam paused. "I didn't know who else to call."

Fair enough, I thought, but her apology did little to soothe my irritation.

"What's wrong, Cam?" I asked, hoping it was something simple like she'd locked herself out of her office and hoped I had a spare key. I did unless she'd changed the locks. Cam had just bought the weekly *Grapevine* newspaper from my grandmother, Rose Mackenzie. She'd moved into an apartment over the paper in a building next door to my diner and hadn't made many friends yet. So, this early morning phone call made sense.

But when she hadn't broken the silence on her end of the phone, I sat up a bit straighter, curious. "Cam? Are you okay?"

She whispered, "It looks like someone's trying to break into your diner."

That got my attention. "Call the police, Cam. I'm on my way." I threw off the covers, upsetting Pip as I jumped out of bed. But she quickly recovered, keeping up with me as I ran around my bedroom, gathering up my clothes.

Normally, I'd linger at the view of the morning sun peeking above the ocean, but today, I was too distracted with the worry of someone possibly ransacking my pride and joy. Pip ran to the door, ready to head outside for our morning jog on the beach. I sighed, sorry to disappoint her.

With an uneasy feeling settling in my chest, I

couldn't enjoy the beauty or indulge in our daily routine. "No time for a jog, Pip," I said, pulling on jeans and a comfy Little Dog Diner T-shirt and grabbed a fleece vest.

Our normal routine consisted of a stretch on the patio, a jog on the beach, then, if I had time, tea and a muffin with Rose before heading to the diner.

"Rose," I called and knocked on the door to her attached apartment. I needed to let her know what was going on.

"Rose?" I said again as I opened the door and peeked inside.

My grandmother, always up early, sat on her couch holding her favorite mug with her cat Trouble curled in her lap. "Come on in and watch the sunrise with me," she said. "It's especially beautiful this morning."

"No time. Cam called and said someone tried to break into the diner."

She swiveled toward me. "What? Call Maggie. This is right up her PI alley. She'll love to dig into it. But remember, sometimes Cam creates a problem just so she has something to write about. I bet it's nothing."

My grandmother stood up and stretched, letting out a deep sigh and acting totally unflustered while I wanted to dash off and check on the diner.

"Make yourself tea while I get dressed. It'll only take me a couple of minutes. Did you call Luke? He'll want to know, too," Rose said over her shoulder as she sauntered toward her bedroom.

Hurry, I wanted to say, but Rose moved to her own timer. Instead, I calmed myself down and said, "Luke's coming home today," without telling her I hadn't called Maggie yet. "Let's check out the diner first, then I'll decide, but you're probably right. This is most likely Cam's overactive imagination. I don't want Luke to worry and rush home for nothing."

I felt slightly better. The police would get there before us, and it was their job to deal with a break-in anyway. Wasn't it?

"Good point, Dani," came Rose's muffled response.

I assumed she was pulling a colorful blouse over her head.

"You know how your regulars check if you're in even when you're closed," she added, her words clear now. "Hoping for a freshly baked blueberry muffin? Cam doesn't know those people yet. And she is jumpier about nothing than just about anyone I know."

I relaxed. Rose was right.

Cam had moved here from Connecticut, supposedly in search of a different lifestyle. She claimed to seek a slower pace, fresh air, sunshine, some local Maine flavor. But before the ink was even dry on the bill of sale, she jumped straight into her new journalist role. It was fair to say her style didn't go over well with the locals. Her prying questions rankled the Misty Harbor residents, who were, shall we say, slow to embrace change.

Rose, for example, had owned the *Grapevine* for years and, at the end, still had to coddle information out of the locals for her stories. So, Cam barging in with her new ideas went over like a smelly fish on the beach.

Without any sense for how things were done in Misty Harbor, Cam totally missed the local signals, subtle or otherwise, to back off and give people space. She would have done herself a favor if she'd slowed down and made small talk before digging up dirt on local businesses, but she said that wasn't *her* style. I guess *stubborn* was her middle name.

At least the Little Dog Diner escaped her scrutiny, so far. Not that there was interesting dirt to dig up anyway. Only delicious food loved by the locals. At least, in my opinion.

Cam didn't know the town's habits yet and coming from the Hartford, Connecticut area, she was used to a faster pace that included more problems than we had in Misty Harbor. At least that was what I hoped.

While I waited for Rose, I called Maggie. As soon as her sleepy voice mumbled, "Hello," I said, "Get dressed. Cam called me. Someone was trying to break into the diner. I'll meet you there in fifteen minutes."

I heard a yawn.

"With coffee?"

"Sure." I hung up before she requested a complete

gourmet breakfast. She'd get it, of course, but I'd wait to hear the particulars of her needs once we were at the diner.

Maggie Marshall, the only private investigator in town and a good friend, had recently moved from the apartment now occupied by Cam to a small caretaker's cottage nearby. She loved having an ocean view, but the interesting thing about Maggie was her relationship with Misty Harbor Detective AJ Crenshaw. It created interesting complications when they found themselves on similar investigating missions, so living away from the center of town afforded her more privacy from the nosy town folk.

While I waited for Rose, I made myself a travel mug of mint tea and gave Pip a small bowl of her chicken and rice mixture. I was just about to pop a pod into the coffee machine when Rose walked in from her apartment, holding two coffees.

"Maggie will need a big black coffee to get her brain in gear," she said, knowing Maggie's dislike for early rising. "She'll also want food. What's the plan for that?"

The sun streaming in the window promised a bright day ahead. I tightened the lid on my tea, and shoved sunglasses on my head. "Once we make sure nothing is actually wrong at the diner, I'll fix us all breakfast. I'd planned to spend the morning baking for tomorrow anyway, so this early start means I'll have an early finish. Win-win," I said, finding the silver lining in my early wake-up call.

Rose pulled a tie-dyed bandana from her big tote and tied it around Pip's neck. "There you go. Can't leave naked," she said, hitching the tote on her shoulder. Then she raised a finger in the air and turned her attention to me.

Had she forgotten someone might be breaking into my diner?

"Dani, I've been thinking. Now that I don't have the *Grapevine* anymore, I have time to help in the diner again. It'll be like old times. Remember when I was in charge and you and Lily helped me? What do you say about that?"

Those were the good old days. So much had changed which wasn't necessarily bad, just different. But hey. I was on a mission, even if my beloved Rose wasn't.

I grabbed the keys to my dark green MG. "Really? I suppose you could help wash dishes," I teased. "Isn't that how you broke us in?"

She snatched the keys out of my hand as quickly as a snake strike, casually tossed them in the air. She caught them before I had time to react. "You know, I think I'll repossess this cute little car, Danielle. And maybe Sea Breeze, too. You and Luke can find another place to live. Don't worry, Pip, you can stay here with me and Trouble."

"What?" I screeched and tried to grab back the keys

without success. For someone in her seventies, Rose was not only spry but clever.

Upon hearing her name, Pip gave a hearty yip, then rushed to the door. She knew what those keys meant, and she loved riding in the MG. But did she understand Rose's silly plan? I doubted that.

I laughed. "You drive a hard bargain, Rose. I guess you could make a double batch of your lemon donut holes. They're always a hit. And I'll clean the pans."

She tossed the keys back to me, handed me one of the coffees for Maggie, and said, "I knew you'd see it my way, dear. Listen, I'll be right behind you, but when I get to town I'll stop in at Cam's apartment and see what the heck is going on with her. It just doesn't make sense that anyone was trying to break into the Little Dog Diner."

I hoped Rose was right.

Chapter Two

I SHRUGGED INTO my fleece as Pip and I walked outside. The cool September air felt invigorating. Pip jumped into the MG and took up her place on the passenger seat with her front feet on the dashboard where she loved watching the world whizz by. Her yip let me know she was glad to be off on an adventure.

"Me, too, Pip," I answered. "I only hope it's a false alarm at the diner."

I pulled out between the granite pillars and headed into town, glad to have the road to myself. I turned up the radio and sang along with the Beatles blaring "Good Day Sunshine."

When Maggie's cottage came into view, I spotted her standing on the side of the road, flagging me down. This wasn't part of the plan, but of course, I pulled up to a complete stop.

She bent down to window level. "I forgot to turn my lights off last night, and my car battery is dead as a beach rock."

This didn't sound like Maggie's normal on-top-of-everything habit. She must have been distracted, but I didn't want to ask if it was related to her, at the moment, rocky relationship with Detective AJ Crenshaw. I didn't want to be in the middle of that drama.

"Hop in. Pip won't mind sharing," I said.

The stop lasted long enough for Rose to fly past. She honked and waved but didn't slow down even though she had way more room in her boat of a Cadillac.

Maggie settled on the seat. Pip danced on her legs and gave her a big lick.

"*Ewww.* Enough, Pip!"

"Don't hurt her feelings, Mags. Here." I pulled out the coffee I'd wedged between the seats. "Rose made this for you."

After a slug and a sigh, she asked. "I needed that. So, what's going on at the diner?"

"Not sure. Hopefully, it's just Cam's wild imagination. She's suspicious of everyone and sees danger in every nook and cranny." I rolled my eyes and wondered if the newcomer would ever get used to Misty Harbor's more relaxed way of life.

A black blur darted into the road.

"Stop!" Maggie screeched.

Instinctively, she tightened her hold on Pip and braced herself against the dash at the same moment I slammed on the brakes. I swerved, tires squealing, to avoid hitting a dog. My heart raced out of control from the adrenaline surge, but at least the dog was safe, and so was my MG.

"What the heck? Whose dog is that?" I asked as I jumped out of the car. I crouched down and extended my hand. "Come here, pup. It's okay."

The dog, a young black Lab, as far as I could tell, came right over, tongue lolling and tail wagging, as happy and carefree as could be.

I searched for a tag but nothing. "No collar?" The answer came in the form of soulful brown puppy eyes.

Maggie and Pip followed right behind me. Pip, always thrilled to meet a new pretty much anything, immediately went down in a play bow. The new dog took one quick sniff, and then they were off, chasing each other in circles at the edge of the road.

"We'll have to take him with us," I said.

Maggie eyed the two-seater. "Do you plan to leave me on the side of the road to make room?"

I snorted at her suggestion. "Someone will pick you up, or you can all squeeze onto the front seat. It'll be cozy," I said. "For you."

She shook her head and laughed like a good sport. "What's better than one Pip on my lap? Pip, plus his newest buddy! My kitty will hate all this dog smell on my clothes, though."

I waited while Maggie managed to squish her lanky

frame onto the seat with Pip on her lap and the new pup sitting on the floor under the dash. It had to be uncomfortable. At least I had my seat all to myself. As soon as I'd pulled onto the road, the new dog wiggled his way up, giving Maggie a good face washing, then squeezed between Pip and the door with his head out the window. Maggie wrapped her arms around both dogs and managed to turn her head enough to see me in the small space behind Pip's head.

"Get going before I change my mind and jump out. My legs are going numb, and I think this guy just tooted. Please hurry, Dani."

When I hit the gas, the tires spit gravel and squealed. Pip yipped. The new pup barked. Maggie put her head back and howled. The only reaction I came up with was laughing at the crazy scene in the seat next to me.

Fortunately for Maggie, it didn't take long to reach the Little Dog Diner. I pulled in behind Rose's Caddy. What surprised me, though, was to see so many cars parked on Main Street so early on a Monday morning. Word must have gotten out about the break-in, which troubled me.

"AJ's here," Maggie snarled. "And Detective Winter."

Uh-oh. Maggie's tone was definitely not, *I'm thrilled to see him.* It sounded more like *I might rip his head off if he looks at me.*

"Well, yeah," I said as if I hadn't noticed her attitude. "I told Cam to call him since it is their responsibility to check on this type of thing. Let's see what's going on."

Maggie didn't budge. "You go. I'm staying right here," she said like a stubborn two-year-old having a mini tantrum.

I twisted in my seat until I faced her. The new pup tried to jump out the window with Pip squeezed next to him, so they were both stuck half-out and half-on Maggie's lap.

"What's going on, Mags?" I asked tenderly.

She was hurting, and she was my friend.

"It's that new Detective Winter. AJ is always talking about Jane this and Jane that. It's driving me crazy, Dani. I'm just not sure I can live with this other woman in our relationship, you know what I mean?"

I reached over and took her hand. "I know what you're saying, and I know AJ cares about you, Mags. But Jane is his work partner, and you are his life partner."

Her eyes opened wide. "Life partner? Don't give him more credit than he deserves. He hasn't popped that question yet, and if he asked today, I'm not sure I'd say yes."

Oh boy. This was the lowest I'd seen Maggie.

Pip finally managed to wiggle out the window with the black pup right behind. Rose walked toward the

MG, and I gave Maggie's hand another squeeze, letting her know she had my support. "Mags? Let's put this on the back burner for now. You need to go catch that dog before he runs into the road again. And I have to find out if there was a break-in attempt. If there was, I'll need you to do some investigating for me." I hoped the lure of a crime would pull her out of her funk. It usually did.

Without replying, Maggie opened the door and whistled. Surprisingly, the black pup stopped and ran right back to her. I hoped he was enough of a distraction from whatever was going on with her relationship with AJ.

I slid out and surveyed the scene around my diner. Why on earth were all my friends' cars parked on the street?

Rose scooped Pip into her arms. "Cam isn't in her apartment or her office. At least she didn't answer when I knocked. Why don't we just go into the diner and have breakfast, okay?"

I glanced at Maggie. "Want breakfast, Mags?" Food always perked her up. For someone so thin, nobody would guess she was a bottomless pit. It must be her high metabolism or all the worrying she did about AJ.

"Food? Yeah, sounds great, and I think this guy is hungry, too." She nodded her head at her new best friend, the black pup. He's kind of boney, don't you think?" She leaned down to the pup's eye level. "Are you hungry, Bones?"

She'd already named him? Not a good sign, in my opinion. "Bring him inside, Mags. You do know that we'll have to look for his owner, so don't get too attached."

"What if he doesn't have an owner?" she said wistfully, leading me to believe my warning was too little, too late. "Come on, Bones."

He woofed, and Maggie smiled. "He already knows his name."

We trooped to the door. Me first, followed by Rose with Pip, and Maggie with Bones.

What a morning.

Chapter Three

WHEN I OPENED the Little Dog Diner door, I stopped in my tracks. What met my eyes made no sense.

Rose put her arm around my shoulders and whispered, "Keep moving, Danielle."

My feet moved, but my brain was frozen until everyone inside shouted, "Happy Birthday, Dani!"

I felt my cheeks heat with a blush of embarrassment. Of course, I remembered that it was my thirtieth birthday, but I'd assumed I'd celebrate with Luke when he got home. How didn't I see this coming?

And there was Luke, all handsome smiles, pulling me close and kissing me. I inhaled his piney, ocean fragrance and sighed.

"Surprise!" he whispered.

"What about the break-in?" I asked, still trying to process this confusing morning.

Rose kissed me on the cheek. "No break-in, Danielle. Luke tasked me with getting you here, so I asked Cam to call you. I left it up to her what she'd say. I expected her to say she'd locked herself out or something innocent like that. Sorry if her ruse caused you worry, but all's well that ends well, right?"

Maggie, with Bones at her side, was now leaning against AJ. Our eyes met and she shrugged and mouthed the word, *sorry*.

I rewound all the little details—early morning phone call about a break-in, Maggie's dead battery, so I'd pick her up, her sob story about AJ to distract me from overthinking about all the cars parked outside the Little Dog Diner.

"Was the dog part of the plan, too?"

"Bones? No, he's just an unexpected surprise," Maggie said, protectively keeping her hand on his head. If the owner showed up to claim him, she'd be one miserable friend.

Lily, my best forever friend, handed me a steaming mug of tea, my travel cup forgotten in the car. Her blue eyes twinkled, and her blonde braid fell casually over her shoulder.

"Your favorite, Dani." The peppermint aroma soothed me from my initial shock to a feeling of gratitude.

How couldn't I love having my friends here with me in my diner? Okay, maybe the plan was a bit over the top, but it certainly worked if surprise was the goal.

Sue Ellen, who had the biggest heart of everyone in the room, sashayed over in a beautiful red dress. "This wasn't my idea, Dani. I offered to come over this morning and drag you out of bed with an offer of taking you out for breakfast at Lily's Blue Moon Inn, but everyone else nixed that plan. They said you'd figure out what was going on."

She was right about that. Surprising me at Lily's Inn would have been way too obvious. "Thanks, though, Sue Ellen. I'll take a rain check."

She grinned and clapped her hands. "Perfect. I get to spoil you twice!"

Luke steered me toward a stool at the counter. "Take a seat, Dani. Lily made blueberry muffins for starters. Then, she has a big breakfast buffet planned for everyone. Rose is helping her in the kitchen, so you don't have to do a thing." He leaned close to my ear. "I hope you like the surprise. I wasn't positive when Rose ran it by me."

"Maybe not at first, but yes, I love it. Thank you." I helped myself to a muffin, one of my favorites, especially since the blueberries came from Luke's blueberry farm, the best in Maine as far as I was concerned.

Luke sat next to me, leaning his shoulder against mine. I felt warm and happy. No, make that perfectly content. "What's with the dog Maggie brought in?" he asked.

I shrugged, unable to say anything without spewing muffin crumbs all over the counter.

"He looks like he could be one of Luna Miller's Labs," he added.

I swallowed, took a sip of tea, then said, "The Labrador breeder? Are you sure?"

"No, not sure, just saying it could be." Luke split a muffin in half and ate a quarter.

"I found him running loose on Oceanside Road. Ran right into the road. After I stopped, he was more than happy to hop right into the car with Pip. Maggie already named him. Bones." I rolled my eyes. "It didn't take more than three minutes for her to fall in love with him. I'm worried that it will break her heart when the owner shows up."

Luke looked pensive for a moment, then said, "Do you know Thorne Waite? He has an apartment off Main Street. I saw him walking a dog that looks just like Bones." I took what was left of Luke's muffin while he continued. "Thorne's okay. He's kind of full of himself. I heard he had a run-in with Cam about something. Not sure what."

"That's no surprise. Cam's had run-ins with just about everyone in town. She certainly isn't making any friends," I said.

Just then, Lily came out of the kitchen. "Attention, everyone," she said, loud enough for the entire crowd to hear. "Breakfast is ready. The birthday girl goes first." She plopped a purple crown on my head.

I swiveled around on the stool just as the diner's door jingled, and Bones let out a bark that rattled the windows.

"Speak of the devil," Luke whispered in my ear. "Cam Carter must have heard us talking about her."

I snorted. "No way."

Her short platinum hair had the just-got-out-of-bed messy look, and she had on fuzzy purple slippers. Odd that she hadn't gotten dressed before barging in, but maybe she was so frazzled she forgot.

She looked from person to person until she zeroed in on AJ. "I need to talk to you. I think it was Thorne Waite who was lurking around this morning, rattling the diner's side door. I called Dani about it." She focused on me as if somehow her problems were all my fault. "Plus, I think someone was walking around in my office."

Rose and I glanced at each other. Did someone really try to break into the diner?

Bones and Pip ran over to her and sniffed her slippers as if they were some sort of wild creature to either snack on or play with.

Cam stepped back and pointed at Bones. "He was here earlier, too."

AJ ran his fingers through his hair as if it helped him digest Cam's words. To be honest, I was having trouble making sense of it myself, but I knew one thing—my birthday breakfast just went from carefree to confusing.

"Bones! Come here!" Maggie said. To the Lab's credit, he loped over to her and sat at her feet. Pip on the other hand, yipped at Cam until I scooped him into my arms.

"Sorry. I'm guessing you aren't a dog person," I said. Not everyone was, a fact that mystified me, but whatever.

"What does that have to do with anything?" she said indignantly. "Someone has terrified me, and you're wondering if I'm a dog person? I'm a journalist, and there's something fishy going on with Thorne Waite. I plan to get to the bottom of it. I'd like to know where he suddenly got enough money to make an offer to buy the *Blueberry Bay Grapevine* from me?" She pointed her finger in my face as if I knew the answer.

AJ took Cam by the elbow. "Let's go to your office and talk about this. We'll let these people get back to their breakfast." He took one long look at the platters of food on the counter as he escorted Cam to the door.

Maggie jogged behind him. "I'll save some for you, AJ," she shouted before she closed the door. As she watched him walk away, her mouth dropped open. "But not one crumb for Detective Jane Winter," she muttered to me. "Look at her, standing over there by the cars, all smug and cute. I can't believe it. She just wiggled her fingers at me."

"Oh, Mags," I said, trying to defuse the situation. "Don't let her get under your skin like that." I pulled her away from the window. Actually, I tugged her. She'd planted her feet and refused to move. "Chin up. Don't let her win, Mags," I hissed in her ear.

But she still didn't move. The three, AJ, Cam, and Detective Winter, disappeared inside the Blueberry Bay Grapevine office. I shrugged, turned away, and left Maggie to her misery. At least Bones stayed right at her side, already loyal.

Luke handed me a plate and together we headed to Lily's feast. I helped myself to her breakfast quiche that featured a crispy potato crust topped with a cheesy egg mixture and bacon. I couldn't resist reaching for a cinnamon roll, still warm and sticky with frosting. The whole buffet made my stomach rumble with anticipation.

"I hear sirens," Maggie said. "An ambulance just pulled up. I'm going over there to see what's happening."

"Great," I muttered to Luke. "Here. Take my plate. I'd better go with her, so she doesn't do something to get herself locked up."

"Take the cinnamon roll and your tea, Dani," Luke said. "Actually, take two because you know Maggie will steal yours." He grabbed a napkin and plopped the two biggest cinnamon rolls on top. "I'll follow you as soon as

I get some coffee."

I raced to catch up to Maggie. Pip yipped at my heels, excited for an adventure, but I was filled with dread that this adventure was one I'd rather avoid.

Chapter Four

OUTSIDE, I GRABBED Maggie's arm, accidentally jerking it a little too hard, but managing to slow her down. Bones danced around her legs, practically tripping her. She faced me, spitting nails or maybe bullets.

"Listen to me, Mags. If you march up to that front door and get in AJ's way, you'll have a bigger problem on your hands than Detective Jane Winter." I wasn't sure that was true, but it got her attention. "You know he hates it when you stick your nose into his work. Come around to the side of the building before he sees you. We'll make a plan. Out of the way," I stressed.

Rose was at my side with her don't-argue-with-me look. "That is my building, and I'm going in whether AJ likes it or not. You two wait out here."

Finally, the corner of Maggie's mouth twitched. "I want to be just like your grandmother when I grow up," she whispered after Rose strode off. "She doesn't take a teaspoon of seagull poop from anyone."

I didn't disagree. We walked to the stairs leading up to the apartment over the Blueberry Bay Grapevine office, the apartment that Maggie had lived in for about a year before she moved out of town. The apartment that Ms. Camilla Carter now occupied. Maggie slumped down on the bottom step, and Bones licked her face. I leaned on the railing and handed her a cinnamon roll, then I bit into the other one.

"I still have a key to the apartment," Maggie said in a conspiratorial tone. "Cam's inside the office with AJ. How about we go into the apartment and use the back stairs down to the office."

"And what? Sashay in like we're crashing a tea party and say something like, oh, never mind us, we're only here to eavesdrop and snoop around? Really? No! That's a terrible idea, Mags. We'll wait here for Rose to find out what she can."

Bones leaned against Maggie. She stroked his head and tussled his ears. The dog couldn't get enough of Mag's affection, and to be honest, Maggie couldn't get enough of his soft fur. Pip wiggled her way onto Maggie's lap, the jealous attention-hog that she was. At least they distracted Maggie from her current obsession with breaking and entering and possibly her previous obsession with Detective Jane Winter. As far as I could see, these dogs possessed a special brand of magic.

"Mags? Do you really think there's something going

on between AJ and Jane?" I had to ask and get this mess out in the open and hopefully talk sense into her if that was even remotely possible.

Her head dropped. "I don't know. AJ talks about Jane all the time. All the time, Dani. It drives me crazy. I mean, she's attractive. How can he not notice that?"

I crouched in front of my friend. "Look at me."

She did.

"You're gorgeous. Sea green eyes. Sophisticated haircut that frames your face in a casual but sexy way. You're strong and athletic. Also, you're an ace shot. I heard Jane's shooting ability is, let's say, subpar."

Maggie snickered, obviously proud of her skills.

"Jane has nothing over you. Sure, AJ works with her. It's okay if they're friends. The thing is, Mags, if you act jealous and don't trust him, you'll risk pushing him right into her welcoming arms." I gently tucked a chunk of hair behind her ear and softened my tone. "If you love him, give him space to be himself, Mags. Don't suffocate him."

She nodded. "Makes sense. Can I do that, though? Back off? In case you haven't noticed, backing away isn't my strong suit."

We both snorted.

"On the flip side, if it doesn't work, I'll find someone else, flirt up a nor'easter and make him jealous!" She looked at me with a big grin. "Just kidding."

Was she really? But I didn't say anything more. As far as I was concerned, I'd said all she needed to hear. Besides, Rose was headed in our direction with a no-nonsense, grim expression. What had she discovered? I braced myself for bad news.

Without any lead-in, she dropped a bombshell. "Thorne Waite was murdered in the *Grapevine's* office. Someone stabbed him. From what I heard, the killer used Cam's letter opener. Straight through his heart."

I gasped. "Gruesome." I felt sick to my stomach and wished I hadn't eaten the cinnamon roll.

"AJ told you all that?" Maggie said incredulously, not fazed by the goriness of Rose's news. "He never shares one morsel with me." Frustrated, she folded her arms over her chest.

Rose bowed her head in a moment of silence and, I imagined, to compose herself. "No, Maggie, AJ told me nothing. I walked in like I owned the place, which I do very well. Confidence is the key. Plus, a bit of luck that AJ was talking to Jane and had turned their backs. No one paid any attention to me because they had their heads down with work. Sometimes, it pays to slow down instead of barging in all hot-headed."

Maggie did a big eye roll. Did she get the message? Maybe. Not that she'd easily change her ways, though.

"I also heard some other interesting information," Rose said. "Thorne's half-brother, Gary, arrived all hot and bothered. He was looking for Thorne's dog. He said Thorne asked him to pick up the dog for a walk while Thorne talked with Cam about something important."

"What kind of dog?" I asked, my stomach sinking like a sailboat in a storm.

Rose looked at Bones. "A black Lab. Thorne got the dog from Luna Miller, the dog breeder. His name is Sherlock."

Bones cocked his head, regarded Rose for a moment, then wagged his tail.

"Sherlock Bones?" Maggie said. "Well, that's quite the moniker for this beautiful boy. But I'm not giving him to this Gary guy. How do we know he's telling the truth? I mean, Dani saved him from certain death when he was running loose on Oceanside Road." An exaggeration that I didn't bother to point out. "That has to count for something." She pulled Bones right onto her lap and held him so tight I knew she'd never let him go without a fight.

"Calm down, Maggie. Gary said he really doesn't want the responsibility, and he's glad the dog disappeared. There might be some kind of adoption process you'll have to follow, but don't worry about that now. AJ has his hands full with a murder investigation."

Maggie lurched to her feet, fire burning in her eyes. "Adoption process? AJ wouldn't dare take Bones away from me. You know what he said when he saw Bones at the diner? He told me that the dog was perfect for me—handsome and super smart. He could already read my every need as if we'd been together forever."

I turned at the sound of footsteps. Uh-oh. AJ headed our way. His sunglasses hid his eyes, but his jaw was clenched, and his fists curled. Not a good sign.

When he was about five feet away, he stopped, shook his head, and said, "Why am I not surprised to find the three of you lurking here?"

Maggie pulled herself tall and said, "I don't know, AJ. Maybe because we're concerned about what happened right next to the Little Dog Diner?" Her tone challenged him to an argument.

But AJ held up his hands and backed off a couple of steps. "I understand that one of you"—he indicated Rose with a flick of his head—"overheard what happened in the *Grapevine's* office. Keep the details to yourself, or whoever let you saunter inside will lose his job. Understand?"

Rose nodded.

Maggie glared and protectively kept her hand on Bones.

I thought about the breakfast I was missing.

"And," he continued. "About the dog. I'd like you, Maggie, to take care of him. It will be temporary pending any claim on ownership."

"But…"

"No buts. That's the best I can do."

Maggie clenched her jaw and mumbled under her breath. Something to the effect of, "We'll see about that."

AJ pretended he hadn't heard, but I could tell this whole business with Maggie and Bones bothered him.

"I sent Camilla to wait at the diner in case I have more questions for her. As you can imagine, she's really shaken up." He opened his mouth like he planned to say something else but changed his mind. Probably for the best, considering Maggie's foul mood. Without another word, he returned to the Blueberry Bay Grapevine office.

"Well," Rose said as if that was that, but it really left a lot unsaid.

"You know what this means, don't you, Dani?" Maggie asked.

I wracked my brain to figure out if she was talking about Cam, AJ, Bones, the murder, or something else completely. Maybe breakfast? I decided silence was my best option. Maggie would blurt out whatever she was thinking anyway.

Rose saved me. "It means we're going back to the diner to enjoy Dani's birthday breakfast buffet. I'm starving."

Finally, someone said something sensible. "Great idea," I said as my mouth watered at the thought of Lily's amazing spread.

"And find out what Cam knows about Thorne Waite," Maggie said. "I have to stay ahead of everything affecting Bones."

I saw all kinds of potential pitfalls looming between Maggie and AJ.

But that was her problem, not mine.

Right?

As we trooped toward the diner, a shiny object on the ground glinted in the sunshine.

"What's this?"

I picked up a round silver-looking object. Perhaps a pendant that had once decorated something? Without another thought, I slipped it into my pocket.

Chapter Five

AS SOON AS I stepped inside the Little Dog Diner, aromas swirled and blended into a sweet, cinnamon and bacon deliciousness. The counter, covered with platters of eggs, bacon, sausage, muffins, fruit, and more than my brain could take in, seemed enough to feed the whole town of Misty Harbor. That was an exaggeration, but maybe the food would serve as a distraction from the gruesome event next door.

Luke rushed to my side, and his strong presence calmed me instantly. "Sorry I didn't come outside, but when AJ escorted Cam in here, he told us all to stay put. What the heck is going on?" He put his arm protectively around my shoulders.

Right. Cam. I glanced at her sitting in one of the booths. Her hair disheveled, shoulders slumped, staring at nothing. Her hands wrapped around a mug in front of her next to an untouched muffin. Bones made a beeline to her spot, tail wagging in a friendly greeting, but she scooched as far away as possible. Undeterred, he wiggled under the table and stuck his head on her lap. Pip followed and jumped on the seat to offer support. Somehow, they knew Cam needed unconditional dog affection.

"You'd better go over there, Dani," Luke whispered. "She wouldn't talk to any of us."

"Okay, but first things first." I grabbed a plate and stacked it high with some of everything until it looked like I was in a circus juggling act.

Luke chuckled.

"What?" I said defensively. "I'm hungry."

"I'll bring you tea."

Carefully balancing my plate, I slid into the booth across from Cam.

She looked up, her eyes dull and listless, then shook her head. "I don't understand what happened."

I nibbled a piece of crispy bacon then used it to point to the muffin in front of her. "You'd better try the muffin, or you'll hurt Lily's feelings."

She looked at it as if she hadn't noticed it was even there until that moment, but she took my advice and sampled it. The bite perked her up. "This is delicious. Must be why this place is so popular." She finished, licking the tips of her fingers, too.

"It's a diner. People come for the food," I said and chuckled at her puzzlement.

Cam and I sat in silence, enjoying our food. She

dabbed her lips to clean off a few remaining crumbs, then sipped from her mug. Coffee, I assumed.

"What am I supposed to do?" Anguish filled her voice and tugged at my heartstrings.

Sure, she'd annoyed plenty of folks in Misty Harbor with her abrasive and tactless ways, but I knew firsthand what it was like to see a body. The image of Thorne Waite would be seared on her brain forever.

"How about you start at the beginning. You're a journalist, so you have a better eye for detail than most people, Cam. Don't leave anything out, even if it seems insignificant. What happened first thing this morning?" I asked.

I continued eating and waited for Cam to start talking. There was no point in pushing her. She had to do this at her pace. I hoped, once she started talking, it would help her work through the trauma and bring back important details. Finally, she sighed deeply and relaxed against the back of the red booth with her arm wrapped around Pip. He happily settled on her lap and gave her chin a lick for good measure. Bones, not to be outdone, wiggled his way onto the seat and leaned against her. I wasn't too surprised that her earlier distaste for dogs had disappeared, considering Pip's adorable cuddliness and Bones's squirmy puppy cuteness.

Luke brought over a mug of tea. "Need anything else?" he asked, raising an eyebrow, and nodding toward

Cam.

She swiveled her head toward the counter. "What's the story about all the food over there? Isn't this place closed on Mondays?"

Sue Ellen, who'd been uncharacteristically quiet until this point, marched toward us, no longer able to contain herself. She swept over to the booth in all her red glory, face set and arms open wide. "It's Dani's birthday today. Your office fiasco threw a monkey wrench into our plans, you know. The least you could do is think about someone else for five minutes."

Cam's jaw dropped. Her shocked expression revealed that she wasn't used to being spoken to so sharply.

To her credit, though, she quickly pulled herself together. "I forgot," she said as if truly upset. "Rose asked me to get you here this morning for your birthday celebration, but the intruder…" Her words trailed off.

I reached across the table and patted her hand. "It really shook you up, didn't it."

Her eyes got misty, and a little hiccup escaped. "I left Connecticut to get away from this kind of stuff, rebuild my confidence, start over. I keep wondering if someone followed me here." She looked at me with eyes that searched for an answer.

"I don't have that answer, Cam, but we'll help you get through this. Everyone in the diner—Rose, Maggie, Lily, Sue Ellen, Luke, even Pip, and Bones. And, of course, me. You don't have to face this alone."

"Thank you," she whispered. After a quick finger comb through her short platinum-blonde hair, she straightened her spine and said, "Can I have some of that food?"

I laughed. "Help yourself. I'm sure Lily made enough for one more person, right, Lil?"

Before Cam had a chance to slide off the bench seat, Lily was on her way with an overflowing plate. "I thought you might need food. In my opinion, it always helps us get through anything."

Sue Ellen reached into her pocket, pulled out a handful of dog treats, and lured Bones and Pip away from stealing Cam's food. "Come on, you two. Leave Cam alone for five minutes."

Rose, squeezing around Sue Ellen, offered Cam a fresh refill of steaming coffee along with some advice. "You won't find better friends than the people right here in this diner. Of course, honesty and respect are required to keep them on your side."

It sounded like a warning to me, but Cam nodded and shoveled a big forkful of egg-in-a-hole into her mouth. At this point, she'd probably agree to anything, but was she trustworthy? Time would tell. This was as good a time as any for a direct, important question.

"Cam," I said. "Did you kill Thorne Waite?"

She sputtered, covering her mouth. Yet she managed

to swallow without choking. "No!" she insisted, eyeing all of us as if we had stabbed her with Lily's breadknife. "That's exactly what worries me. If you think I killed him, how will it look to the police? I mean, he was murdered right under my nose in my office. And worse than that, I had a terrible argument with him yesterday."

"About what?" I asked.

"Well, it's embarrassing, but he came to my office, and his dog pooped on my walkway."

"Bones? He's still a puppy, you know. He obviously needs more training," Maggie said, defending the dog who'd stolen her heart.

"Fair enough, and I probably overreacted, but I stepped right in it. My brand new white open-toed strappy sandals—ruined. Never mind the brown muck that squished in between my toes." She grimaced. "I let Thorne know exactly what I'd do if it happened again."

I could imagine the words hurled at him. "Was anyone else around?"

"Ha! No witnesses? That would have been too lucky, right?" Cam looked totally defeated.

I noticed Lily at the counter, nodding. "I saw the whole thing, Dani. It was a pretty strong threat, and under the circumstances..." She raised her hands in a *whatever* gesture.

Cam paused in thought, then took a deep breath and continued. "Thorne's half-brother was with him, a no-good loser as far as I'm concerned. Also, a woman had just parked in front of my office and stood on the sidewalk. I thought she planned to head toward my office but changed her mind after my confrontation with Thorne." She shrugged. "There were probably other people, too, but those two I distinctly remember."

Cam pushed her plate away and slid out of the booth. She wandered around and stared out of the window. "I feel like a prisoner in here."

Rose joined Cam and put an arm around her waist. "We all need a distraction, especially you, Cam. Luke? Is it time?"

"Time for what?" I asked.

Luke pulled me out of the booth and plopped something on my head. Before I could blink, Lily walked out of the kitchen with a big fruit pizza covered with candles. "Happy birthday, Dani!" she said.

I gasped in surprise. "Oh, my. That's beautiful. Too pretty to eat," I said, even though I didn't mean it for a minute.

I'd had Lily's fruit pizza before, and it made my mouth water. How could it not with a sugar cookie base covered with her special whipped cream cheese blend, topped with fresh strawberries, sliced kiwi, and blueberries.?

"Big breath and a make a wish," Luke whispered.

I did. I wished AJ would find Thorne's killer quickly

without sucking me into the investigation. A birthday girl could hope, right?

I blew on the candles, but one stayed lit. More bad luck.

Then someone rattled the side door, banged on it, and rattled the doorknob again.

Chapter Six

BONES CHARGED THE door, barking, ready to slay the monster trying to enter. Pip followed, no less intimidating, considering her size. I wondered what the commotion was about.

"I'll take care of this," Luke said as he rushed past me, quickly reaching the door and opening it.

Luna Miller, a woman a little older than me, tried to push past Luke. She came into the diner occasionally, but I never liked her vibe. This morning, she stood out with her blonde ponytail, baseball cap, and black t-shirt with the logo LUNA'S LABRADORS in silver letters.

"This is a private party. The diner is closed," Luke said with an arm on each side of the door. I grinned when I saw he had effectively blocked her from getting a foot inside.

"I'm looking for my dog," she announced as she craned her neck and peered around Luke into the diner. She pointed to Bones and said with authority. "There he is. Come here, Sherlock."

It didn't take an experienced sleuth to see she meant trouble.

Sherlock, or Bones, as I'd already gotten used to calling him, slunk under the table, hiding at the spot where Cam and I had been sitting.

"Bones? How do you figure he's *your* dog?" Maggie said with disgust dripping from her voice.

Luna let out a shrill cackle. "Bones? The dog I just saw is Sherlock," she replied as if talking to a child. "I sold him to Thorne, and with the situation such as it is"—she paused as if giving a respectable moment of silence—"ownership reverts back to me according to the contract he signed."

Maggie stormed across the diner so fast, she took Luna completely by surprise. In fact, our visitor took a step back and almost tumbled off the step. She caught herself only to be the target of Maggie's finger, jabbing her in the chest.

"I don't think so. Detective Crenshaw appointed me as Bones's guardian because I saved his life when he was running free on the road. If I hadn't saved him, he was sure to be hit by a car. So, how about you mosey on back to wherever you came from so my friends and I can get back to our *private* party." Maggie flicked her hands to get Luna moving.

Luna huffed and sputtered, but it was obvious she wasn't getting into the diner or one step closer to Bones.

"I'll be back." A threat uttered but not taken seriously by any of us.

"Wait a minute," I said, pushing Maggie aside before the door slammed shut. "Did you come by earlier looking for Sherlock?"

Maggie jabbed me in the ribs and sent me a chilling glare, but I just ignored it.

Luna's face softened as if she'd finally found the one reasonable person in the diner. She was happy to be in the spotlight again. "As a matter of fact, I did. I got a call that a black Lab was sniffing around your diner early this morning. At the time, I didn't know it was Sherlock, but after seeing him here, I'm one hundred percent positive. So, are you going to let me take him, or are you still part of this silly power-trip game?" With her arms crossed over her chest and jaw jutting out, she smiled as if she'd aced a test and gained the upper hand.

I stared right back without blinking to let her know I wouldn't be cowed by her stance. "Oh, this isn't a silly game, Luna. As a matter of fact, it's turned into something deadly, as you must know by now. And you can be sure we're keeping Bones." I started to turn away but stopped and added, "By the way, thanks for confirming that you were right here at the scene of the crime."

Her jaw dropped as if I'd physically punched her. That would have been satisfying on some level, but the alternative of slamming the door felt pretty darn rewarding. I hoped it smashed the shock right off her face.

Behind me, the diner fell silent.

I turned around. Everyone stared at me, looking just as shocked as Luna had been. It was only a matter of seconds, though, before Maggie screeched with laughter and wrapped me in her arms.

"Brilliant, Dani! Absolutely mind-boggling! That's why you solve mysteries. You're always a step ahead of everyone else. Probably even AJ, but don't dare tell him I said that. You know what? Bones and I are indebted to you forever. Thanks for being on our team, right, Bones?"

By now, Bones had slunk out from under the table, where he'd hid, scared by the noise, I imagine. Before long, whatever had happened was long gone from his memory, and his bouncy confidence reigned supreme. He jumped on Maggie, demanding her full attention, including a body hug. She released me and happily obliged Bones.

After that drama, Lily's dessert beckoned. I was more than ready for a big slice of her fruit pizza. The perfect fix for any problem, including ridding my mouth of Luna Miller's bad taste.

Lily was ready for the swarm of hungry people waiting for her big triangles of fruit pizza slices she was handing out on plates.

I grabbed one and savored the first bite. The sweet

sugar cookie base, topped with cream cheese, strawberry, and a kiwi slice, tasted like a bit of heaven.

While we ate and chatted, I heard Sue Ellen ask Luke what else was on the agenda for my special day. He grinned and said nothing, much to her annoyance and mine. I'd had enough surprises for one day, but Luke liked his surprises, so I'd just have to be patient to see where else the day went. With any luck, everything else would be fun.

I helped myself to a second slice and plucked a strawberry slice off the top.

"Dani?" Cam asked, interrupting my enjoyment. "That's the woman I saw yesterday on the sidewalk when I argued with Thorne. Her name is Luna?"

"Yeah, Luna Miller, owner of Luna's Labradors."

"Interesting that both Thorne and the person he got his dog from showed up at the same time yesterday. I don't know what it means, but there was tension between them."

I looked at Bones. Did that mean something?

"I hate to bother you again since you've been so supportive," Cam hesitated. "But would you mind coming with me to my apartment? I'd really like to change out of my jammies and find some suitable footwear. I'm a little freaked out to go alone. I know, it's irrational but... would you?" She lifted up her fluffy purple slippers, looking embarrassed that she'd been caught out in something so cozy but unattractive.

I glanced quickly at the mess on the diner's counter, but Luke read my mind and pushed me toward the door. "It's your birthday. You don't need to do any cleanup. I'll help Lily. It's the least I can do since this was my idea." He smiled, pulled me close, and gave me a heart-melting kiss, then whispered, "You're in this whether you want to be or not, Dani. You have to protect Bones or Maggie will totally lose her mind. I suspect that will also put you in the path of AJ's investigation, so tread carefully."

More than anything, I wished Luke and I could walk out and spend the rest of the day snuggled up at home. Looking at the view of Blueberry Bay and listening to the sound of the waves in the background would be the perfect birthday respite. I didn't need extravagant surprises. Don't get me wrong, I appreciated Luke's efforts, but I was fine with simple.

If only I could hide away from this murder investigation, but the plain fact was that Luke was right. I had to help Maggie. And by helping her, I'd be sticking my nose where it was definitely unwanted.

"I'll come. Let's go, then." I snapped my fingers. "Come on, Pip. We're leaving."

Pip dashed to the door, always ready for something new. Bones whined but stayed with Maggie. For whatever reason, he'd decided she was his person. And that was just fine with Maggie.

I opened the door and waited for Cam to walk ahead of me.

Maggie ran over and handed me a bag. "Blueberry muffins. In case you bump into AJ."

"How thoughtful, Mags. You mean in case I need a bribe?"

She gave me a quick hug and whispered, "You never know what's lurking out there. Be careful. Something strange is going on."

Pip had run ahead of me, so I grabbed the bag of muffins and followed Cam. She was barely out the door before I saw Lyndsey Malden from the shop across the street scurrying up the driveway.

"Cam! Ms. Carter! Wait. I need to talk to you."

"Lyndsey?" she said, then under her breath so only I could hear, she added. "Just what I don't need right now."

It was odd that Lyndsey was even here since she worked at Creative Designs for AJ's sister, Kelly. She usually opened the shop.

Lyndsey stopped next to Cam, breathing hard from her run. Her long brown braids swung back and forth as she looked at Cam then at the activity at the Blueberry Bay Grapevine office.

"What an exciting first day for me, right? Want me to interview the detective about the murder since, you know, Thorne and I dated not too long ago? I'm dying to get started."

"About that, Lyndsey." Cam fidgeted, obviously uncomfortable with this conversation. "This changes everything."

I couldn't hold my tongue any longer, especially since Lyndsey seemed way too excited that someone she knew was murdered. "Lyndsey? How do you even already know about what happened?"

She rolled her eyes as only a twenty-one-year-old could who was talking to a clueless older person. For the record, I reminded myself, I'd only just turned thirty. In my book, that didn't even qualify as a slightly out of touch person.

She held up her phone. "Word gets around, Dani. I mean, a murder? It doesn't get more exciting than that, right?"

It depended on your definition of exciting.

Chapter Seven

CAM STILL HAD to deal with her Lyndsey problem before she could walk away to get dressed in a more professional outfit. I imagined she felt about as foolish as a cat stuck in a tree, standing here, almost on Misty Harbor's Main Street, hair disheveled, wearing purple fluffy slippers and heart jammies. This would help push her already questionable reputation with the locals into a laughingstock.

"Listen, Lyndsey," she said, pushing the fledgling reporter out of the public's view, "I know I promised I'd give you a chance working for me, but today is a bad day. I need to deal with this unexpected tragedy. Since my office is off limits until I don't know when, I can't access my notes, plans, contacts, or much of anything at this point. I'll call you." She turned away, effectively putting an end to the conversation.

It sure sounded like a brush-off to me.

Lyndsey stamped her foot. "I don't believe it. She can't just..." And with that, she gave me a long, hard stare. "Just brush me off like I'm a piece of lint stuck in those fuzzy slippers. Can she? She promised. Besides, I know stuff. I knew Thorne. I know there was a problem with his dog." She looked around. "Where is the dog anyway? Did crazy Luna take him back?"

Where to start? I wondered. At the beginning. "Did you quit your job at Creative Designs?" I asked.

"Um. Not exactly? Kelly left for a few days, and Mondays are always slow. It probably has something to do with your diner being closed. I always recommend the Little Dog Diner to customers, especially the lobster rolls. They're the best. Anyway, I thought I'd squeeze in some time with Cam this morning. See if that's gonna work out. I don't want to burn any bridges with Kelly, you know? She's nice and all, but helping customers pick out the perfect gift is a dead-end job. I want something more exciting, you know?"

I did know. Nothing against Kelly, but Lyndsey had a point. I couldn't blame her for looking for a better job, even if I didn't agree with her sneaking off while Kelly was away. But that was between the two of them.

"So, you and Thorne?" I raised my brows hoping she'd share some gossip.

She moved closer to me and put her hand on my arm like she couldn't wait to spill the beans on him. "Did you know he won a million-dollar lottery ticket that he didn't cash in yet? He always bought one ticket a week with fantasies of hitting it big time. I thought it was a waste of money, but I was wrong!"

Okay. I did not see that coming. I shook my head and waited for more.

"I think his sleazy half-brother, Gary, is after the ticket."

Lyndsey was certainly full of information and had no problem spreading it, whether accurate or not. I'd listen but take it with a grain of salt.

I eyed her skeptically. "Wouldn't you like to get your hands on that ticket, too?"

Her face lit up. "Are you kidding? Absolutely! I'd love all that money more than just about anything, but Thorne told me it was securely tucked away in a safety deposit box." She chuckled. "I had to look up what that even was. Thorne said he was biding his time. He always said stuff like that, which never made sense to me. Why not just take the money and have some fun, right? I can't help but wonder, who gets access to that box now that he's dead, right? Smacks of motivation for murder, right?" She lowered her voice. "I love thrillers, and motivation is key, right?"

She paced back and forth. This girl had more energy than a mug of my high-caffeine espresso. And way too many *rights*.

"Where the heck is AJ?"

I saw Cam disappear up the stairs and heard her

apartment door close, but I couldn't tear myself away. If Lyndsey had more to spill, I wasn't about to miss the opportunity to hear it. "What's the deal with Sherlock?"

She turned back to me and bunched up her eyes, almost as if she'd already forgotten I was standing a few feet away from her. "Who?"

"Sherlock. Thorne's dog."

"Oh. That's his name? I never paid any attention. Once Thorne got that dog, he didn't have any time for me. It was always, *I have to walk the dog*, or *I have to get home to feed the dog*. Who wants that inconvenience in their life, right? Not me. I saw the writing on the wall in big black letters and told him I had better things to do with my life than compete with a dog for his attention. Best decision I ever made, right?"

Apparently, she hadn't noticed Pip sitting right next to me, listening to our back and forth. It was more than apparent that Lyndsey noticed Lyndsey and not much else when she had an agenda.

"Oh. There's AJ coming out of the Grapevine office. I don't need Ms. High-and-Mighty Camilla Carter to give me permission to talk to the detective. He has to talk to me since I practically run his sister's store."

She honored me with a wink like we were big, best buddies now, then scurried off to bother AJ.

Phew. I was exhausted after listening to Lyndsey, but she did share some interesting tidbits. The question was, were they true? I headed toward Cam's apartment, but AJ cut me off with Lyndsey right on his heels.

"Dani?" he called. "Did Camilla Carter leave the diner?"

Lyndsey stopped a few feet behind AJ with a big grin on her face, as if she expected to hear some juicy dirt coming her way.

"She went to her apartment to get changed out of her pajamas, AJ. I'm going up there now."

He relaxed a little until he glanced over his shoulder. "Lyndsey? What are you still doing here? I told you to get back to Creative Designs. You have a job there, or did you forget? Kelly won't like to hear about you gallivanting around while she's gone. You're supposed to open up her store."

"But..."

"No buts, Lyndsey. This is a crime scene, and you need to leave. Now."

She walked away slowly, glancing back every couple of steps, probably hoping to hear anything AJ said before she crossed the street.

He pulled me toward Cam's apartment and out of Lyndsey's earshot. "Listen, Dani," he said quietly. "I don't want Cam doing some kind of disappearing act back to Connecticut or someplace else. I have questions for her. You're already aware of the fact that a murder took place in her office. It's no secret that she had a big argument with the victim yesterday. I need to know more about all that. Understand?"

"Of course." I offered him the bag of muffins.

His hand twitched, but he didn't take it. "I know you. Is this a bribe?"

I smiled as sweetly as possible, annoyed by his comment, even if it was sometimes the case. "Of course not. I'm only the messenger. These are from Maggie. She wants to thank you for asking her to take care of Bones." I touched his arm. "That dog means everything to her, AJ. It's like they bonded the minute he jumped into my car and onto her lap. If anyone takes him away, well, I don't know what she'll do."

He nodded. "I get it. Tell her not to worry about Bones. I'm responsible for him at this point, and I trust Maggie to take good care of him." He took the muffins and smiled. "Tell her thanks, too. And tell her to quit worrying that there's something between me and Jane. We're work partners. That's where it ends, but Maggie doesn't understand, and it's putting a strain on me. I don't know how to handle the jealousy thing, Dani."

"Are you serious about her, AJ? I mean, really, truly for the rest of your life serious?"

He nodded, and his mouth opened with understanding. "You mean, put a ring on her finger?"

I shrugged. "I'm not telling you what to do, AJ. You're the only one who knows if she's the one and only for you."

Was I out of line with this comment? I didn't know and didn't really care. At this point, something had to be done to break Maggie's tendency for jealousy before she drove me out of my mind. If that meant nudging AJ to propose, then so be it. Apparently, he was oblivious to the obvious solution. On the other hand, what if AJ decided she wasn't the one? I hoped I hadn't started the beginning of the end of their relationship.

I sighed. Sometimes my role as peacemaker was more complicated than I wanted.

"Did you hear me, Dani?"

I shook myself out of my stupor. "Huh? Oh, I guess not. What did you say?"

"Have you heard anything about Thorne coming into a lot of money?" AJ bit into a muffin, swiping at the crumbs spilling down his shirt.

He must be looking for a motive, just like Lyndsey suggested. "I did, but I don't know if it's true."

He made a circle motion with his hand while he ate, gesturing for me to continue.

Did I want to share this tidbit? "You deal in facts, not hearsay, AJ."

He finished the muffin and glared at me. He wasn't moving until he got the information out of me.

"Talk to Lyndsey," I said. "By the way, how's the muffin?"

AJ looked off into space, deep in thought. "Delicious as always. Thanks. Go check on Camilla before she disappears, okay?"

"What's that supposed to mean? Why are you so worried about her? What do you know?"

AJ grinned. "You know I can't tell you about my investigation, Dani. Oh, and for the record, I don't believe for a second that Maggie sent out these muffins. That's not her style."

"Really?" Furious at him now, I grabbed the bag back. Maybe Maggie would be better off without AJ in her life after all. He didn't understand her very well.

"Forget about another muffin, AJ. I gave you my advice about Maggie, so make a decision. I'm done being in the middle of you two." I started to walk away, then stopped and turned back toward him. His hand was still in the same position as if the bag was still there. He looked shocked.

"Oh, and for the record, don't expect me to share what I hear if you aren't willing to give a little in return."

"That's not how it works, and you know it," he said, obviously surprised and annoyed by my action.

I couldn't care less.

I turned back toward Cam's apartment, glad for a destination.

Sure, I didn't know her well, but I had a feeling that was about to change. If helping her meant helping

Bones, I was all in, but I'd be darned if I'd help AJ with his investigation.

He was on his own.

I stomped up Cam's apartment stairs, unloading my frustration with each step. Who did AJ think he was? First, he tried to wheedle gossip out of me, then he insulted Maggie, one of my best friends. Sure, it was no secret that she and much of anything domestic didn't pair well, but she was smart, loyal, and beautiful. She had probably watched the whole exchange through the window, too.

Pip dashed past me, tail wagging, excited as always. That helped my mood. It was always the little things that helped, right? Like a trusty companion, a beautiful view, or an unexpected gesture like a bag of muffins. Unfortunately, thinking about a bag of muffins brought me full circle back to my anger with AJ. At the moment, I didn't think he deserved Maggie.

I knocked on Cam's door, tapping my foot impatiently as I waited for her to let us in. What took her so long?

Did she flee?

Chapter Eight

CAM FINALLY OPENED her door. I sighed with relief. I shouldn't have let AJ's words pollute my belief about her because I didn't think she was a flight risk. She struck me as someone who would want to clear her name. Her biggest issue now seemed to be that she was in the wrong place at the wrong time.

"Come in," she said as she poked a dangly silver earring through her ear. "I'm almost finished dressing." Then she rushed back into her bedroom.

Pip and I wandered inside. The apartment, one I'd been in many times when Maggie lived here, had a completely new feel. Cream-colored walls brightened the room and provided a background for a crisp gallery of framed photos. I stepped up for a closer inspection. The high-quality close-ups of flowers, distant panoramic ocean views, and several portraits were a snapshot of Cam's interests. I hadn't been aware of her obvious talent before, but it paired perfectly with her journalism career.

The rest of the living area held a few pieces of furniture, probably not antiques but tasteful and well-loved. The only thing missing to make the space perfect, at least in my opinion, was a cat curled on the sofa or a dog greeting us with a wagging tail. But the shelf of plants in her window brought color and a different type of life into her space.

Cam emerged in gray slacks, a cream-colored blouse, and a flashy pink scarf twisted around her neck. For someone in her fifties, she obviously took pride in her appearance, both with her well-toned body and elegant clothing.

"I needed that quick shower to wash away the tension from this morning," she said. "Seeing that guy lurking around trying to break into my apartment and your diner really threw me for a loop. Then, walking into my office with the detective and finding..." She shuddered instead of finishing her thought.

I patted her shoulder. "Try not to think about that, Cam. Now is the time to figure out the why instead of dwelling on the ugly moment." I noticed an address book next to a basket of keys on a small table. "Who has access to the Grapevine office?"

She pursed her lips, and her forehead wrinkled. "I haven't changed the locks yet, so you and your grandmother, Rose? Misty Harbor seems safe enough. I liked the idea of you two as backup in case I ever locked myself out. I get distracted sometimes when I'm in the middle of an interesting story, and locking myself out was a definite possibility." She laughed, sounding embarrassed for revealing that personal trait.

I didn't tell her that any number of people could have gotten hold of a key over the years. Rose, never a stickler for locking the door, could have unwittingly allowed almost anyone to come in and grab a key. Who or why? I didn't know but still a possibility.

"Earlier, you said you argued with Thorne. Was there more to it than stepping in his dog's poop on your walk?"

Her eyes flashed with anger. "Jeez. Is this an interrogation?"

I held my hands up in what I hoped was a calming gesture. "Hey. I'm only trying to help. AJ will ask these questions and more, so you should be prepared."

Her shoulders relaxed, and she said, "Yeah, yeah, you're right. Sorry." She swept her short platinum hair away from her face, more at peace with me now. She gestured for me to take a seat while she took care of some last-minute tasks.

"It's just, well, I moved here to get away from this type of stuff. Reporting on a small town's festivals and awards, that kind of thing, seemed like the tonic I needed for this stage of my life instead of all the drama that surrounded me every single day in the city. But murder? Right under my nose? Making me a suspect? I never saw that coming!"

I grimaced in agreement. "No one ever does, Cam. Are you ready to go back to the diner? AJ asked you to stay there, but once he's finished questioning you, you can stay with Rose if you'd like to. That is, if you're not comfortable being alone here."

She slipped on a lavender suede jacket and slung a black leather tote across her chest, looking more city businesswoman than Misty Harbor local. I imagined she'd get the hang of our ways sooner or later.

"Thanks for the offer. I'll think about it. I hope I can get into my office as soon as possible. Get back to work. That's what I need at the moment."

Pip, always curious, had spent the last fifteen minutes sniffing around the apartment. It was so tidy that I didn't expect her to find much of interest.

Cam slipped her feet into a pair of black leather flats that looked comfy as long as she didn't plan on taking a hike on the beach. Pip darted over and dug at the rug where her shoes had been. The edge rolled into a clump, revealing a folded piece of paper.

I picked it up and handed it to Cam.

"What's this?" she asked, flipping it over in her hand, then unfolding it, reading it, and handing it to me.

I skimmed the letter silently, then read it out loud. "Ms. Carter. Meet me downstairs. I need to talk to you. Luna Miller is up to something with her dogs. Sorry about Sherlock pooping on your walk. That wasn't how I wanted our meeting to go. I'll wait in your office. The door's unlocked. TW."

I folded it, and since Cam didn't ask for it back, I stuck it in my pocket for safekeeping.

She stood in front of me, frozen in place, all color drained from her face. "What does that mean?"

"Did you meet Thorne in your office?" The question had to be asked.

"What? No! Your dog just found that note. I never saw it before. Thorne must have shoved it under my door this morning when he was sneaking around."

"Okay. Do you have any details about what he wanted to tell you about Luna's dogs?"

She shrugged. "No idea, but this is going from bad to worse," she said, sounding defeated.

I opened the door and waited for Pip and Cam to walk out ahead of me, then I followed, closed the door, and checked that it was locked. It was. I didn't want to be the reason her apartment was left open to vandalism if that was on someone's mind.

We started down the stairs, Pip running ahead of us. "Listen, Cam," I said. "Put your journalist's hat on. There's a story here, and you know it has to be connected to Thorne's murder."

Cam kept her head down, focusing on the stairs.

"He said something was up with Luna's dogs and,

earlier, she stormed into the diner demanding Sherlock be returned to her. Why? You were there. Use your talents and start digging."

Cam needed something to focus on besides the body she saw in her office. Maybe this was it.

"Okay," she said, brightening a bit. "I'll call Luna. Tell her I want to interview her for a story, that it will be great free advertising," Cam said, formulating her plan as we stood on her stairs.

"Perfect, but if you go, don't go alone."

"Why? You think *she* killed Thorne?" Cam continued down the stairs toward the diner where Pip had bounded ahead. She sat now, wagging her tail, waiting for us.

"I have no idea, but someone murdered him, and if he actually knew something bad about Luna's business, my guess is that she wants to keep it secret. I'd certainly put her on a suspect list," I said. "And one more thing, Cam. Thorne said the *Grapevine's* door was unlocked. What do you make of that?"

"I always lock it. I'm positive."

"Interesting. That meant either Thorne had a key, or someone else unlocked it and was waiting inside for him."

Before we could say anything more, I opened the door to the diner, savoring the lingering aromas from my birthday breakfast feast. Bones bounded over to greet us, and Luke looked up from wiping tables. His smile warmed my heart.

"Perfect timing," he said. "Cleanup is done."

"Darn. I was hoping you'd leave a pile of pots and pans for me to wash." I snickered, then kissed Luke on the cheek. "Did I tell you that I'm over the moon that you're back?"

"I don't think so," he whispered in my ear, sending shivers down my spine.

"Well, then. I couldn't have been happier to see you when I walked into the diner this morning. Thanks for planning this feast. You know, it caught me completely by surprise, and you know I don't love surprises, but this? Perfect."

"Except for the, you know…" He nodded his head toward the *Grapevine's* office.

"Yeah, except for that."

Luke put his arm around my waist. "Don't forget, Dani, I had a lot of help." He always downplayed his efforts and shared the praise with everyone else. A noble trait.

Maggie stuffed her cloth in her apron pocket and rushed over to me. Bones jumped up on her thigh, looking for treats or affection; I couldn't tell which. From his happy demeanor, I think he'd take either.

"AJ came in looking for Cam," she said. "He acted like he wanted to tear something apart when I told him she wasn't back yet. And he didn't say anything about the muffins. Did you give them to him?"

Oh boy. Here I was, in the middle again. "Listen, Mags. I gave AJ the muffins, and you know what he said to me? He didn't believe they were from you. That it wasn't your style. So, I took them back and told him he doesn't deserve you. That's my honest opinion." No point beating around the bush with one of my best friends.

Her nose flared. She clenched her jaw. Her eyes turned to a stormy sky color. "You probably think I'm mad at you for that, but I'm not. I'm glad you took them back. He would have shared them with you-know-who anyway." Her hand stroked Bones's head. "I have Bones. I don't need AJ."

I didn't see that reaction coming, and if Maggie meant it, good. I didn't believe it, though.

Maggie looked at Cam and asked, "Now, what's the plan?"

I pulled the note out of my pocket and let Maggie read it. "Cam wants to interview Luna for a story about her dogs. Maybe do a little digging. Get some leads to follow. Find out what's going on with her business."

Maggie nodded. "As a private investigator, I'll add my stamp of approval. It's a good place to start, but don't visit her alone. Is there someone you can take with you?"

"Are you offering?" Cam said hopefully.

"Probably not a good idea. Luna would be suspicious right off the bat. I have Bones now, and she probably knows I'm an investigator. I should stay in the background on this."

I was impressed by how focused Maggie sounded. Maybe pushing AJ to the back burner was the best thing for her at the moment. He always distracted her.

"Okay. I'll ask Lyndsey. She's a really motivated young woman, and I promised to give her a tryout. Plus, I feel bad that I brushed her off earlier, but she caught me when I wasn't thinking clearly. I'll make it up to her. Ask her if she has time to come with me when she's done with her shift at Creative Designs. That is if Luna will see us." She smiled and nodded. "Yes. I like this plan. Thank you, Dani. You helped me get my head straightened out. You're a lifesaver."

I didn't agree.

Thorne lost his life, and there could be another death if we weren't careful.

Chapter Nine

"OH GREAT," MAGGIE said, making a face. "Here comes you-know-who."

I looked out the side door of the diner just as Detective Jane Winter reached for the doorknob. As far as I knew, she'd been first on the scene after Cam called in her report about a possible intruder in the diner, but this was the first time she'd shown her face to us.

"She looks like she ate a squished toad or something." Maggie sounded pleased about that stomach-churning description.

Jane let herself in, and I wondered when the door had been left unlocked. Nothing to do about that now. The Little Dog Diner was busier than Grand Central Station this Monday morning even though, technically, we were closed.

Jane stepped inside with her confident I'm-in-charge expression. I suspected she hoped it conveyed a level of intimidation, too. Her gaze stopped on Cam, and it seemed to have the desired effect. She squirmed uncomfortably.

Jane pointed to one of the booths "You. Sit down over there." She snapped her fingers at Mags. "And how about a cup of coffee and a muffin."

I cringed when I looked at Maggie, not sure what she was about to do. But Maggie was always full of surprises. "Sure thing, Detective," she said in her sweet and completely fake voice. "Coming right up."

I watched as Maggie drained the coffee pot of the last half cup of leftover, lukewarm coffee. She added a partially eaten muffin to a plate and brought both to the detective. I stifled a laugh.

"Here you go. Just leftovers. It's all I could scrounge up." She started to walk away, then stopped and turned back toward the detective. "Didn't Detective Crenshaw share the blueberry muffins I sent over earlier?"

Nothing like sticking the knife in and twisting it.

Jane leveled her eyes on Maggie. "I didn't see any muffins, and I'm sure he would have saved one for me."

Maggie flicked her wrist dismissively. "I guess it slipped his mind." She walked away, but I could see her shoulders twitching like she was trying not to howl with laughter.

"Ms. Mackenzie? Over here, too."

I slid in next to Cam and reached under the table to pat her thigh, guessing she had no idea what to expect. I didn't either, but I refused to let Jane get to me.

Jane pointed her pen at Cam. "Who called in a possible break-in?"

"I did?" Cam said like she really didn't want the attention but couldn't run from it. "I saw someone sneaking around and trying the doorknob of the diner early this morning. I called Dani to let her know. She said to call the police, and she'd be right in."

Jane jotted in her notebook, sipped her coffee, made a face, and took a piece of the muffin.

"Did you go outside to investigate? Talk to the person. Find out anything?"

"No. I was scared. I basically locked myself in my bedroom and didn't leave my apartment until I saw activity here at the diner."

Jane tapped her pen on her notebook. "What scared you?"

"The person sneaking around."

I expected to hear Cam add *duh* to her answer.

"But why? Did you think that person was up to no good?"

"Yeah, I did. That's the point. That's why I called it in. I wanted someone with authority to figure out what was going on." Finally, Cam found her voice and stood up to Jane.

"I see. You're a journalist. Is that correct?"

Cam nodded.

"As a journalist, isn't it important to get the story

before anyone else?"

Cam slapped her hands on the table. "I don't believe this. I don't put myself in danger for a story. I'm not reckless."

Jane seemed frustrated that her questions hadn't completely rattled Cam, but I decided it was because Cam wasn't hiding anything. Jane leaned back and stretched her legs under the table, bumping against me.

Then Jane turned her eagle eye on me. "Ms. Mackenzie, when did you arrive here at the Little Dog Diner?"

I was used to Jane, so I didn't let her rattle me. "I don't know exactly. I was delayed after Cam called because I saw a dog running loose on the road. I caught him, and then I guess we arrived around sevenish? It turns out my husband"—I turned and smiled at Luke—"had planned a surprise birthday breakfast for me. It was kind of chaotic with food and conversation. Then, Cam came in looking for AJ."

"You mean Detective Crenshaw?"

"Yes. Detective Crenshaw." I tried not to roll my eyes.

"And?" Jane indicated I should elaborate.

"And AJ went to the *Grapevine's* office with Cam," I said, reverting back to his name to annoy her.

Jane glanced around the diner. "Okay. You arrived, and there were people here. A party. Did anyone see the person that scared Camilla? The person who allegedly tried to break into the diner?"

Rose came over to the table. I was impressed she'd waited so long. "I asked Cam to call Dani and get her to the diner for the surprise birthday breakfast. We thought Cam's phone call was her way of getting Dani here."

"Rose Mackenzie, right?" Jane said and continued jotting in her notebook.

"Yes, we've met before. Just to be clear, everyone here came for Dani's surprise breakfast."

Jane checked her watch, then pushed herself out of the booth. "Who arrived first?"

Pip took the opportunity to snag the empty bench seat across from Cam and me and sniff at the remains of Jane's muffin. She rejected it.

Lily, who tended to stay out of the limelight, walked out from behind the counter, wiping her hands on a dishcloth. "I arrived first, around five, I think it was, to bake the muffins and finish all the last-minute stuff I couldn't prepare yesterday."

"Lily Lemay, owner of the Blue Moon Inn, right?"

"Yes, that's correct. Dani and I were partners here at the Little Dog Diner before I branched off on my own. I have my own key and use this kitchen every once in a while, if I need more space than I have at my inn." Lily leaned against the counter between Rose and Sue Ellen.

Together, they looked like an impenetrable wall. I

was glad they were on *my* side.

Jane sat sideways, her butt on the edge of a booth table. One leg planted on the floor, and the other dangling casually. Although, nothing about her was casual. I sensed every question, every movement, was deliberate with the intention of intimidation and catching someone in a contradiction, probably Cam.

"So, Lily. You were here when Camilla said she saw someone trying to open the diner's door. Did you hear anything?"

"No. But I like to listen to music with my earbuds when I'm baking. Once I'm in my zone, so to say, not much disturbs me. I was preparing a lot of food and wanted it to be finished by the time everyone arrived. That was my focus."

"Or maybe there wasn't anyone checking the doorknob." Jane looked back at Cam. "Maybe Camilla made it all up."

Cam tensed next to me. "Why would I make it up? I saw what I saw."

I squeezed her arm and shook my head when she looked at me, hoping she'd stop talking.

"When Cam called me, she sounded very frightened," I said. "I told her to call the police. I had no reason not to believe her."

"And yet," Jane said. "Rose already stated that she asked Camilla to call you with some sort of ruse to get you to come to the diner for your surprise breakfast. Which makes me wonder if you, Camilla, killed two birds with one stone—fulfilling Rose's request and sending the police on a wild goose chase after a nonexistent person to take the focus off you."

Cam gasped.

Detective Winter smiled and continued before anyone had a chance to argue. "Moving on, what time did everyone else get here?"

I slid out of the booth and stood facing Jane. "Accusing Cam of lying is totally uncalled for. Have you checked for fingerprints, canvassed the area, do all those detective things you're supposed to do?"

"In good time, but I also look at every angle, and if you don't like it, I guess that's why I'm wearing the badge, and you aren't." Jane turned away from me. "So, when did everyone else arrive?"

No one answered.

"Fine, doesn't matter," Jane said. "I came as soon as Camilla called the station. I didn't see anyone lurking around, but I did see Rose, Sue Ellen, and Luke arrive at seven. AJ right after, and Dani and Maggie about fifteen minutes later. Everyone went inside without a care in the world. Everyone, that is, except Camilla. You arrived disheveled about ten minutes after that. Which left plenty of time to go down that back stairway into your office." She slapped her notebook against her open palm.

"Something doesn't add up, and believe me, I'll get to the bottom of this mess."

I didn't like the assumptions she'd made, and to be honest, as in the past, I couldn't find much of anything to like about Detective Jane Winter.

She could do her investigation any way she pleased, but it wouldn't stop me from helping to find the killer to clear Camilla's name if she was innocent. But I also had another interest in this case. More importantly, keeping Bones with Maggie. Just looking at that sweet face and those innocent brown eyes as he leaned against Maggie's leg made my heart flutter with worry.

As soon as Jane left, it seemed as though the whole Little Dog Diner sighed with relief. If that was even possible.

Camilla faced us, straight as a tall oak tree and just as strong. "If any of you have any doubts, I did *not* kill Thorne Waite. I'm convinced he was killed because of something he uncovered. I'll dig until I find it, and then, you know what? I'll rub Detective Winter's nose in that pile of poop. And enjoy every minute."

I believed her.

Chapter Ten

LUKE, PIP, AND I snuck out of the diner while the others consoled Cam as best as they could. As far as I was concerned, they didn't need us. Besides, not to sound whiny or anything, it was my birthday. At the moment, all I wanted was time alone with Luke. He'd been away for a few days setting up some deals to sell blueberry-related items at the next blueberry festival. It seemed so far away, but he said the planning had to be done now for next year's festival. At least that step was done.

I drove to Sea Breeze, our home overlooking the beach that ran along Blueberry Bay. The house had belonged to my grandmother Rose, but she had bequeathed it to me several years ago with the understanding that we share it. After Luke and I got married, Rose insisted on her own space so she wouldn't be in our way. It seemed silly to me since Sea Breeze was big enough for all of us, but Luke designed and built a cozy apartment with a private entrance for her and her cat Trouble off the patio.

Luke followed me home in his truck. As we got closer, Pip whined and tap-danced on the seat. She knew exactly where we were, and she loved the beach as much as I did. Maybe more.

I pulled my MG into the driveway, and Luke parked next to me. As soon as he slid out, he asked, "Straight to the beach? Or do you need a snack?"

I laughed. "More food? You've got to be kidding. Lily outdid herself, and even with all the interruptions, I ate too much."

Luke put his arm around my shoulders. "Good. Our beach walk will burn off the extra calories and make room for lunch."

I groaned. "I'm not too sure about that. I might need to skip lunch to make room for dinner."

We walked inside where the ocean breeze filled the house with a piney, salty scent. The peacefulness almost wiped away the morning's horror. Almost, but not quite.

"I can use a cool drink before we head to the beach. How about you?" Luke asked.

"Iced tea out on the patio sounds perfect."

Luke filled two glasses with my berry blend iced tea, added a squirt of lemon, and grabbed a handful of dog treats. Pip, impatient to get outside, scratched at the French door until I opened it.

"Ahh." I sighed when the sun hit my face. "Now I

can actually relax and enjoy the day with you and Pip, my two favorites. It's all I need."

"Yoo-hoo!"

I dropped my head into my hands at the sound of Sue Ellen calling. "Luke, I love her, but now? Can't we even have ten minutes alone?"

In response, he squeezed my hand and rose to greet our friend.

Pip, on the other hand, was thrilled and yipped her excited greeting as she ran to Sue Ellen when she appeared around the side of the house.

"Good," she said in her loud, effusive voice. "You're here. I saw your car, but the front door was locked. I was afraid you'd be somewhere down on the beach."

That had been the plan, and part of me wished we hadn't stopped to enjoy the iced tea. The other part knew that there had to be an important reason for Sue Ellen to show up, so I swallowed my frustration and sipped my iced tea. I was determined to enjoy my drink, at least.

Sue Ellen took Luke's arm, and as she hurried over to me, her dress sailed behind in a cloud of red. She plopped down next to me. "You won't believe it, Dani. Lily found something just after you two left," she said, slightly out of breath from her dash around the side of our house.

She reached into her giant tote and pulled out an envelope. "Here. Take a look at this."

"This isn't some sort of birthday surprise, is it? Like a spring-loaded snake or something that's going to startle me?" I looked at Luke. He shook his head and raised his hands in an I-don't-know gesture.

I opened the clasp on the manila envelope. It looked empty.

"Here," Sue Ellen said impatiently. She grabbed the envelope back and shook something into her hand. "We think Thorne slipped this under the front door of the diner, but it was hidden under the mat until Lily moved it to sweep." She handed me a small envelope. "Look inside."

This whole situation felt creepy as if she'd delivered a message from the great beyond, but I opened the small envelope anyway. Inside, I saw what looked like a lottery ticket and a note, which I read out loud.

"I don't know what else to do but leave this with someone I believe is one hundred percent trustworthy. I'm afraid my life is ruined and possibly in danger because of this stupid winning ticket and some information I've discovered that I want to talk to Camilla about. If something happens to me, please donate the money to an organization that helps dogs in some way. I left a photocopy of the ticket and these instructions in my safe deposit box, too. TW."

"Why me?" I asked, looking at Sue Ellen and Luke.

"Why not?" Sue Ellen said as if it made perfect sense to her. "You've proven yourself to be honest and fair over the years. Thorne was desperate for a quick hiding spot, and you filled the bill. I'm not surprised."

Of course, Sue Ellen wasn't surprised. I'd saved her from a killer trying to steal a valuable statue from her home. That earned her undying loyalty, but Thorne? I barely knew the guy.

Luke took the note and read it to himself, then slapped it against his open palm. "This, along with the note Thorne left at Cam's apartment, suggests there could be two different motives, Dani. One is to steal this ticket, and the other is the information he uncovered about Luna's Labradors. Right?"

I tried to wrap my head around this information and make some sense of it. There was no lack of motivation for someone to kill Thorne, and enough people were in the vicinity to be suspects.

"That's one explanation," I said. "But it's possible Luna decided to silence Thorne *and* get the money. Maybe her business is in financial trouble. Maybe that's what he discovered. Cam can dig around in that area."

"If your theory is correct, Luna will still be searching for that lottery ticket," Luke said. "It's unlikely she'll figure out you have it, but we need to find a safe place to keep it."

"Or I could turn it over to the police. I refuse to deal

with Jane, though, so I'll call AJ if I decide to go that route. First, a walk on the beach. I need to think this through more thoroughly." I drained the rest of the iced tea and stood up. "I'll hide this envelope in my safe. I suppose it's as secure there as anywhere else."

Luke nodded, but Sue Ellen looked skeptical.

She shook her head. "I'll think about it while you're on your walk."

It only took me a few minutes to store the envelope with the winning lottery ticket in my safe and return to the patio. "Ready, Luke?"

"Ready." He took my hand. The rough callouses from working all those years in his blueberry fields felt familiar and comforting.

I looked at Sue Ellen. "What about you? Do you want to wait here until we get back?"

"Definitely. I'll hold down the fort. Right here." She slid her chair back a few feet until it was completely under the umbrella, pulled a floppy hat out of her giant tote, and arranged it at an angle on her head. After she pushed her sunglasses into place, she smiled and settled into the chair. "Take your time, you two. No sense rushing into any rash decisions."

Pip was already on the beach as soon as Luke and I started down the stairs. She flew across the sand to the waves, yipping and yapping, following the back and forth of the waves, but somehow managing to keep her feet dry.

Luke put his arm around my waist, and I leaned against him, content.

"This is really all I need to make my birthday perfect, you know," I said this as we ambled along, watching Pip chase seagulls ahead of us. "The beach, the ocean, you, and Pip. I don't need anything fancy."

In response, Luke pulled me closer as if that were even possible.

My bare feet sank into the wet sand. The cool, scratchy sand between my toes always reminded me of my childhood walks on the beach. The icy waves splashed over our feet. Seagulls squawked overhead, and lobster boats bobbed in the bay. It couldn't be better.

As Pip raced ahead, I spied a dog and person walking way off in the distance, probably Pip's destination. She patrolled this section of the beach as if it were hers, greeting everyone like they were long-lost friends.

"That looks like Bones up there," I said.

Luke laughed. "Funny thing about that. All black Labs look alike, don't they."

We continued, swinging our arms, and matching our stride.

Pip and the young black dog ran toward us. The man whistled, but his dog was having none of that. He was having too much fun chasing Pip.

"We'd better pick up our pace and get the dogs heading back in his direction," I said. "I don't want anyone accusing Pip of kidnapping someone's dog."

Pip and her new friend ran a circle around us then streaked back up the beach toward the man. I picked up my pace because I didn't recognize the man and didn't want to risk an awkward confrontation with Pip if the stranger were in the middle of something.

"Watson, you know better than that," I heard the man scold once he had his dog under control again.

"Hello," I said. "Nice day for a stroll on the beach." I aimed for friendly, bending down to pat his dog. "You're enjoying this, aren't you?" I cooed to the dog.

"There isn't a leash requirement?" asked the man.

I waved my hand. "Technically, yes, but as long as your dog is friendly, and I can see he is, don't worry about it. Watson, is it?"

"Yeah, I haven't had him for long, and he's not used to his name yet. At least not when there's something more interesting around, like your dog. I was worried he wasn't coming back when he took off. This morning has been more than I can handle, to be honest. I came to the beach for some fresh air before dealing with a terrible family tragedy."

Luke put his arm around my shoulder in a protective gesture.

"Oh? I'm sorry to hear that." Was he talking about Thorne's murder? I took a wild guess and asked, "Is your name Gary?"

His head jerked up in surprise. "Yes. Do I know you?"

"Maybe you've seen me if you've been in the Little Dog Diner. I own it."

Gary clipped a leash on Watson and held him close. "Right next to the *Blueberry Bay Grapevine*, right?"

I nodded. "That's right. Thorne was your brother?"

"Half-brother," he clarified. "I've been visiting. Thorne and I were discussing a business venture," he paused and swiped at his eyes, "but that won't happen now."

Gary looked out over the bay. Why was he telling me these details?

"I'm so sorry," I said. "You know, when I saw your dog, I thought it was Thorne's black Lab. They look so much alike."

"They do, don't they. They're from the same litter. The police told me someone is caring for Sherlock. It was too much for me to deal with him and Watson." The dog looked up at Gary as if expecting something, maybe a treat.

"Did your half-brother win a million-dollar lottery ticket?" I asked, knowing my question would hit him out of the blue, which was my intention.

The corner of Gary's eye twitched. A tell? "Who did you hear that from, his ex-girlfriend?" he asked with disgust lacing his words.

"That doesn't really matter. I was only wondering because money is always a motive for murder."

Again, that twitch. "Yeah, he did. That's how we were going to finance our business venture, but now..." Gary held his arms out his side. "Lyndsey will probably cash it in."

I wasn't expecting that. "She has the ticket?"

"I don't know, but it makes sense, right? She was always hanging out with Thorne after he won it, then boom, she dumped him. You tell me what that looks like. Come on, Watson," he said and walked away from us toward the Kitty Point Lighthouse.

Once he was out of earshot, I said, "That was an abrupt departure. What do you think, Luke?"

"Well, Lyndsey doesn't have the ticket because Thorne left it with you for safekeeping."

"Right. If Gary killed Thorne, hoping to get his hands on the ticket, Lyndsey could be next."

"You'd better have a talk with AJ."

Luke was right, even though I didn't want to.

Watson kept looking back at us as if he'd much rather stay on the beach and play. I couldn't blame him. After Gary had climbed the trail to the lighthouse parking lot, we turned around and trudged back to Sea Breeze.

Any relaxation I'd gained at the beginning of our walk, gone.

What surprise was in store for me next?

Chapter Eleven

SUE ELLEN WAVED furiously at us from the top of the stairs leading up from the beach.

My stomach twisted into a knot. I grabbed Luke's hand and pulled him toward the stairs. "Something's happened."

We took the steps two at a time behind Pip, breathlessly reaching the top as Sue Ellen flung her arms around me.

"Oh dear," Sue Ellen said, stepping back and twisting her hands together, searching first my face, then Luke's with a worried expression.

I took her arm and led her under the umbrella. "Just spit it out, Sue Ellen. What happened?"

"I don't really know, but Maggie called and mumbled something about taking Bones to the vet and asking me to tell you to meet her there."

"Is he okay?"

Sue Ellen slumped onto the chair behind her and shrugged. "I think so. She said he was acting strange like he was suddenly confused and seemed shaky."

It took a few seconds for this to settle and make sense. "Okay. Luke can stay here with Sue Ellen and Pip. I'll meet Maggie at the Furry Friends Hospital. She's probably a total wreck, but Dr. Addison Philips will figure out what's going on. She's always great with Pip and Rose's cat, Trouble."

Sue Ellen wrapped me in her arms again. "You always come to the rescue for all of us, Dani. You know how much Bones already means to Maggie. Now hurry before she has a complete breakdown." She gave me a little sendoff shove.

Luke had his phone out. "I'll send Maggie a text and let her know you're on the way."

"Thank you," I said, then slipped on my sandals, rushed through the house, and out to my car.

Fortunately, the Furry Friends Clinic was on my side of Misty Harbor, so only a ten-minute drive away. I pulled in next to Maggie's SUV and rushed inside. The receptionist looked up.

"Shelly? Maggie Marshall and Bones?" I asked, hoping she'd give me good news.

Shelly smiled. "I assume you're referring to Sherlock Bones?"

I nodded.

"They're in with the vet. Is Maggie your relative?" Shelly's forehead scrunched in confusion.

"No. A friend."

She jotted something in her scheduler. "Maggie explained what that poor dog has gone through today, and they could both use some support. I'll let them know you're here, Dani."

I paced, hoping beyond hope that there was nothing seriously wrong with Bones.

The door to the back area opened. "You can join them. Follow me."

"Is Bones okay?" I asked.

She opened her mouth, then closed it. "I'll let you hear the diagnosis from the vet."

Diagnosis? That didn't sound good. Shelly opened one of the exam rooms and stepped aside so I could enter. Bones rested on the table with Maggie standing near his head, stroking his ears and murmuring softly while Dr. Philips finished her exam.

"Hello, Dani," Dr. Philips said. "Bones is fine. He had a small seizure. It can be controlled with medication as I explained to Maggie. I diagnosed this about a month ago, and I'm guessing he missed a dose or two, which triggered today's event. Nothing to worry about going forward as long as he stays on his meds."

"You already knew about Bones's condition?" I asked.

"Yes. Thorne brought him here. Sorry, I have to get used to the new name, Bones. I'm sorry to hear about what happened, and Bones is a lucky boy that you found him when you did."

Dr. Philips lowered the exam table, and Bones jumped off, wagging his tail, and looking no worse for the wear. She offered him a dog bone, and he gently took it from her fingers.

"He's always such a polite boy," she said and patted his head.

"What does this condition mean?" I asked. "Is it something the breeder should be concerned about?"

A shadow quickly crossed Dr. Philips's face. "Yes. I told Thorne to contact the breeder. I don't know her personally, so I left it to him. Any reputable breeder should contact all other people who got puppies from this litter or even another litter from the same parents. It's not something she should ignore."

I glanced at Maggie. She'd clamped her jaw shut, but she said nothing.

"A reputable breeder?" I said, astonished. "And if she's not, is there a chance she'd try to cover it up?"

Dr. Philips finished updating Bones's chart then turned toward us and sighed. "Unfortunately, it happens more than I'd like to admit. Breeders cover up all kinds of things. But Bones here will be fine and will live a long life. Don't worry about him, Maggie. I can tell that the two of you have already bonded. I think Thorne would be pleased that his dog found you."

I leaned against the exam table. "Tell me doctor, was Thorne going to tell Luna, the breeder?"

"I believe that was his plan. Now, it's up to you to make sure she knows. It's possible she does and has followed up with the other puppies. That's something I don't know about." She scribbled something on a notepaper. "Here, give this to her. It explains the problem so she can't deny knowing about it. She can call me if she wants more information or advice. I'm not expecting a call, but I'm always available to help."

Dr. Philips handed Maggie the exam paper. "Take this to the receptionist, Maggie, and make a six-month appointment for Bones."

"Thank you so much! Are you sure he'll be okay? This is all so new to me. I have a cat, but I haven't been responsible for a dog before."

Dr. Philips laughed, a delightful melody that filled the exam room. She patted Maggie's arm. "It's not rocket science. He'll be fine, and you have Dani and Pip to help you get through any rough patches. Labradors want to please. As long as Bones gets plenty of exercise and attention, he'll be a perfect companion. By the way, does Radar get along with him?"

Maggie grimaced. Her kitty, Radar, had been queen of her castle for about six months and probably expected it to stay that way forever. "They haven't met yet. Honestly? The introduction worries me. Knowing Radar, she won't be thrilled."

"Take it slowly and give them time to work out the pecking order. My guess is that Radar will remain queen. Cats have a way of being incredibly intimidating. If I remember correctly, Radar likes to be the boss and if Bones has any sense, he'll respect that. He's still young enough to back off as long as Radar stands her ground." Dr. Philips opened the door. "Good luck, Maggie. I'll see you in six months," she said and disappeared into another exam room.

Maggie looked at me. "I feel awful. I didn't even consider how Radar would react. Does that make me a terrible pet parent?"

"The worst," I said, then laughed. "You're overthinking all of this. Like Dr. Philips said, Labradors want to please. Bones and Radar will do fine. It might take some time, but as long as you let them figure it out, they will."

She nodded but not in a very convincing manner. "I don't know, Dani. Am I making a mistake by taking on this extra responsibility?"

I looked at Bones leaning against Maggie, staring up at her as if waiting for her to let him know the next move. "No. Not at all, Mags. Give it time. Now let's get that bill paid so we can get back to Sea Breeze."

We walked into the waiting area, and Maggie whispered, "I can't believe what Dr. Philips said about Luna. Are you thinking what I'm thinking? Do you think Luna wanted to cover up this defect?"

"It's possible."

"Over my dead body," Maggie said forcefully, which was the completely wrong thing to say, considering what had happened to Thorne. She paid her bill and said, "Let's get out of here."

Before I climbed into my car, I said. "You know, this information about his seizures gives Luna a strong motive to kill Thorne, and if she'd gotten Bones away from you, she could have totally covered up the problem."

"I've been thinking the same thing, Dani. She's dangerous. And we suggested Cam question her."

"Let's drop Bones off at Sea Breeze and visit her ourselves. Just in case," I said.

"Good idea. I know I told Cam I should stay in the background, but this is too important." Maggie let Bones jump into the back of her SUV, and then she followed me home.

This whole situation was becoming more and more dangerous.

Chapter Twelve

BY THE TIME we got to Sea Breeze, it looked like a parking lot instead of a driveway. Rose's Cadillac and Lily's van were parked next to Sue Ellen's giant red Escalade. Luke's truck was way off to the side where he always parked. I squeezed in as far as possible, leaving just enough room for Maggie to pull in next to me. Lily had just about reached the front door but turned around when I pulled in.

Apparently, Pip heard my car, too, because, by the time I got out, she came flying around the corner of the house, yipping her greeting. No doubt she'd stuck in a few complaints about being left behind, but when she saw Bones, I knew from her slobbering smile all was forgiven. He distracted her with a game of chase back to the patio. Nothing like being scolded, then relegated to a second-class citizen by a feisty terrier.

When I caught up to Lily at the front door she asked, "Did Sue Ellen give you the envelope?"

I nodded. "Yes. It's in my safe for now. Until we figure out the best course of action."

"What's to decide?" Lily asked. "Cash it in and donate it to an animal shelter. That's what Thorne requested."

"I want to talk to a lawyer first. Just in case someone else has a legal claim to it."

"Like his half-brother? I met that guy at the diner. To be honest, Dani, he seems slimier than a rotting jellyfish."

I chuckled as we walked inside. "Interesting description. When Luke and I bumped into Gary on the beach, I sensed he was hiding something. Oh, I almost forgot. He had a black Labrador with him."

Maggie stopped and stared at me. "What? You didn't tell me that."

"His name is Watson. He's from the same litter," I added.

"I wonder if Watson has the seizure disorder."

Lily held up her hands. "Slow down, you two. Seizure disorder? Maggie, is that why you rushed to the vet?"

"Yes." Maggie explained what had happened to Bones because of missing his medication. "And remember how Luna wanted to take Bones when she saw him at the diner? Do you think she knows?"

By now, we'd walked onto the patio where everyone else had congregated. A platter with cheese, crackers, and fruit was on the table next to a pitcher of what looked like lemonade. Thanks to Rose, I assumed. Ever the hostess.

"Knows what?" Rose asked. "Are you talking about Bones? Is he okay?"

I watched as Bones followed Pip at top speed down the stairs to the beach. They reached the sand, turned, and charged back up. He sure didn't act like anything was wrong with him.

"Before I explain everything, I need something to drink," I said and poured myself a glass of tangy lemonade.

"Okay," I said after guzzling the cold drink. "To catch you all up, Bones is fine. He has a seizure disorder that's controlled with medication, but Dr. Philips thinks he missed a dose or two. Maggie noticed he'd begun to act odd, so she took him to the vet. Her quick thinking prevented another seizure, and now he's back on the medication."

"The thing is," Maggie said, taking over the story. "Luna should inform everyone else with a puppy from the same litter. Also, she shouldn't breed those parents again. If she's a reputable breeder."

"Is she, though?" Sue Ellen asked. "Come here, Bones. You poor baby. I have something for you to help you get over your traumatic experience." She retrieved two of her special sweet potato treats from her giant tote and held one out for Bones and the other for Pip.

"My honest opinion?" I said. "Thorne discovered the problem. When he confronted Luna, she wasn't happy about it. Maybe she refused to do anything. Thorne went a step further and decided to talk to Camilla, hoping she'd write an article and expose the disorder. At least, that's what I think happened."

"Something like that could ruin her business," Rose said. "Quite the motive for murder, right?"

"Exactly. When Luna came to the diner this morning, I think she had every expectation that she'd walk away with Bones. Who could have predicted that Maggie would bond with him and take charge in such a short amount of time. I doubt Luna ever expected Maggie to stand up to her." I put a chunk of cheese on a cracker and popped it in my mouth.

"So, now what?" Luke asked. He put his arm around my shoulder like a protective shield. I leaned into his strong embrace, knowing he'd always be there to help in any way possible.

"Dr. Philips gave Maggie a note explaining about the disorder for her to give to Luna. We're going to visit her and see how she responds."

"I'll come, too," Luke said in a tone that left no room for argument.

"Perfect. Three against one puts the advantage in our court. It also puts her on notice that several people know about the situation, and we won't back down until she deals with it," Maggie said forcefully.

She was hot under the collar about this situation with Bones, and I couldn't blame her. It also worked well as a distraction from her jealousy concerning AJ and Detective Winter, which might or might not be anything at all. The ball in that mess was in AJ's court as far as I was concerned.

"Dani!" Rose said, pulling me from my thoughts. "Maggie should leave Bones here. He'll be more comfortable if Pip stays, too. What do you think?"

"I agree, but Pip won't be happy about being left behind again. Although, they might be ready for a nap after all the morning excitement. I've got a spare dog bed for Bones to use."

I went inside with Maggie tagging right behind me and pulled the extra red plaid fleece dog bed out of the hall closet. I carried it to the living room and put it next to Pip's smaller bed in a sunny spot.

"What do you think?" I asked Maggie.

She moved the bed several inches until it touched Pip's, then she looked at me, and, in a quivering voice, asked, "It looks more and more likely Luna killed Thorne to keep this seizure disorder secret."

I looked out the window at Blueberry Bay. The view of the ocean that went on forever helped keep things in perspective. "Listen, Mags. We don't know for sure yet so let's try to keep an open mind. I know my mind has already headed down that path but let's try to get more information before declaring her a murderer. Don't forget that lottery ticket is a big motive, too, and we don't know if Luna even knew about it."

Maggie stood next to me, arms at her sides as if struggling to stay calm. "Good point. I think worry about Bones is clouding my judgment. Let's go back outside, so I can tell Bones he has to stay here."

I didn't say anything. If Maggie needed to have that conversation, who was I to judge? I talked to Pip all the time.

Bones had made himself comfortable in the shade of the patio table, completely stretched out like he had no care in the world. Pip had made herself comfy in Sue Ellen's lap.

"All set?" Rose asked.

I suspected the question was loaded with much more than the obvious. I nodded, knowing she'd understand I had everything under control. We had that special link of understanding between us.

Lily, who hadn't said much through all this, stood up and brushed a few crumbs off her pants. Even though her long blonde hair hung down in a single braid, loose strands blew around her face. "Dani? I just thought of something."

I patted Pip goodbye, but she barely acknowledged

my gesture. She'd be happy staying here with Rose and Sue Ellen.

"What is it, Lily?"

"With everything that's been going on, I forgot that Thorne's half-brother is staying at the Blue Moon Inn. He booked a week's stay with his dog. He's very chatty and mentioned that he was planning something here in Misty Harbor. Some kind of business venture. Do you think that has any significance to Thorne's murder?"

"That is interesting. Luke and I bumped into him on the beach, and I asked him if he knew whether Thorne had a winning lottery ticket. He admitted that he knew about it, and they were going to use the money for a business venture. He was quick to accuse Thorne's ex-girlfriend of getting her hands on that ticket."

"Lyndsey?" Maggie asked.

"Yes. She works for AJ's sister at Creative Design. The thing is, she told me that Thorne put the ticket in a safe deposit box."

"So, Gary and Lyndsey knew about the ticket. Anyone else?" Lily asked.

"No idea. And I'd like to keep it that way. Especially since I have it for safekeeping at the moment."

Sue Ellen stood up, sending Pip off her lap. "Oh, sorry, Pipster, but I'm going to the Blue Moon Inn with Lily. I hope you don't mind, but I'm not taking no for an answer. I don't want you alone with that half-brother.

Who knows what he's capable of?"

Well, that took care of where everyone would be for the next bit of time.

"Mags, should we let Cam know we're going to Luna's?"

"Nope. She can do her thing, and we'll do ours."

"Okay."

We left in Maggie's SUV, Luke riding shotgun and me in the back. I had an uneasy feeling about how this would go, especially if Maggie lost her temper.

Chapter Thirteen

THE SIGN AT the end of the driveway—LUNA'S LABRADORS—was beautifully stenciled with a black Labrador head over an ocean background. Underneath, the words WHERE PAWS MEET HEARTS sounded welcoming.

"I don't feel like we're intruding," Maggie said after she'd made the turn. Next, we headed toward a white farmhouse with black shutters.

She parked alongside a white van with the same LUNA'S LABRADORS logo on the door. She gripped the steering wheel as if she was preparing for a confrontation.

"Okay. Here's my plan. We find Luna and get in a friendly discussion before I spring the seizure disorder on her. Sound good?"

Luke nodded, and I turned to Maggie. "Are you sure you're up to this?"

She gave me a thumbs-up, but uncertainty filled her eyes. "Yes," she finally admitted, her voice stronger. "I can't let this woman keep selling puppies with health problems. She needs to fix this."

"Great," I said, trying to sound enthusiastic. "Let's find Luna Miller."

I opened the back door and slid out. The three of us stood on the gravel, surveying the area.

"I'd guess that's a good place to start." Luke pointed to a red-roofed structure off to one side and behind the house. It had the same LUNA'S LABRADORS sign above the door.

"You think?" I teased and looped one arm through Maggie's and the other through Luke's. We headed toward the kennel.

"What if she refuses to do anything?" Maggie asked.

"Then it's on to Plan B," I said. "But I think she'll act. Look at us, Mags. Three people who know about the problem, and there could be more. Strength in numbers."

Maggie clamped my arm close to her side. "Good point," she said and picked up the pace.

When we entered the barn, a small bell hanging on a chain above the door tinkled and set off a cacophony of barking dogs.

Once my eyes adjusted to the low light, I saw an extremely clean and organized space. Several pens lined one wall with beautiful black Labradors barking and wagging their tails at us, some jumping on their enclosure. It sounded like a friendly greeting and made me smile. The farthest pen held a handful of puppies, all wiggly with their noses pressed against the wire. I wanted to jump in with them and cuddle each one.

Luna waved from the puppy pen. "Hello and welcome!" She climbed out and headed our way. "I'm really happy to see you."

I wasn't expecting such a warm greeting, and from Maggie's furrowed brow, she wasn't either.

"I totally bungled my meeting this morning at your diner. I'm so sorry. I shouldn't have barged in and demanded to take Sherlock, but I was worried about him."

Luna rattled on, and I wondered if she was hiding nerves or something more sinister. Or could she truly just be worried about Bones?

Luke stepped forward and offered Luna his hand. "Luke Sinclair. I own Blueberry Acres, and I know what it takes to run a business. Impressive place you have here."

Apparently, he was the only one of us who hadn't gotten tongue-tied because he managed to push through our preconceived expectations. His was the perfect response, going a long way to put me at ease. Hopefully, Maggie, too.

"Danielle Mackenzie," I said, following Luke's lead with my hand extended.

Luna warmly covered it with both of hers. "Of

course. I recognize you from the Little Dog Diner and those amazing lobster rolls. I grab one at every opportunity." She turned to Maggie. "And you've taken on Sherlock's care."

"I have. Actually, we made a trip to the vet already."

Luna's expression turned from smiling to worry in a fraction of a second. "Oh no! When I heard a black Lab was running loose and then the news about Thorne's murder, I was afraid poor Sherlock wouldn't get the medicine he needs. Where is he? Is he okay?"

"He's fine. Dr. Philips explained everything to me and got him back on the seizure disorder meds. She's concerned about other puppies in the same litter, though."

"Can we talk while I keep working? My help"—she rolled her eyes—"never showed up, so I've been playing catch-up all day."

"Yeah, yeah." Maggie sent Luna back to work with a flick of her wrist.

While Luna filled a bucket with water, she said, "I've contacted everyone who adopted one of those puppies, including Thorne's half-brother. So far, they're all okay. It seems that Sherlock just had bad luck. Unfortunately, it happens."

She turned off the water and carried the bucket to the first pen. "Come on, Sasha, I know you're dying to come out here and meet everyone." Luna turned to us.

"This is Sherlock's mother. She's the calmest dog I've ever had the pleasure of knowing. I expect he'll take after her."

A beautiful black Labrador, stocky with rich brown eyes that seemed to look right through me, walked over and sniffed each of us in turn. When she reached Maggie, her tail went wild, and she woofed.

"She smells Bones," Maggie said, smiling.

"Bones. What a funny name. He'll always be Sherlock to me," Luna said as she cleaned Sasha's water bowl and filled her food bowl.

Maggie crouched down. Sasha eagerly sniffed every inch of her hands where she'd scratched Bones's ears and her legs where he'd leaned against her.

Luna opened the next pen. "Sasha and Sherlock were inseparable. I'd planned to keep him, you know, because of the seizure problem, but Thorne insisted. That was the puppy he wanted. It took longer than it should have for me to discover his devious plan. He and his half-brother." She stopped working and looked at us as if she'd said too much.

What devious plan was she talking about?

"Anyway, that's why I stipulated in the contract that I'd take him back if Thorne couldn't keep him. But if you're going to take care of him properly, Maggie, I'm okay with that. The best thing for that dog is consistency and a caring person. He'll thrive where he's the main man. You know what I mean?"

Luna didn't wait for an answer. She moved to the next pen and continued her chores. Luke followed, commenting on the kennel's structure. I could tell he was trying to keep Luna busy talking, but she responded to his questions with grunts. Something in her demeanor had changed.

"What do you make of what she just said? What devious plan?" Maggie whispered.

I shrugged. We casually moved closer, hoping to hear more, but Luna had retreated into a silent work mode.

"Luna?" She turned toward me. "This morning, you told us that someone called you and said a black Lab was running loose around my diner. Did you see anyone when you showed up?

She put her water bucket down with a clank on the cement floor and faced us. The gate was still open, and puppies rushed out. Luna barely noticed. I couldn't help but scoop one wiggly black pup into my arms and get rewarded with puppy kisses.

I looked back at Luna, expecting her to round up the puppies. Instead, her face was filled with anguish. "I saw Thorne, but, like a chicken, I left before he saw me. My focus was finding the loose dog, but I didn't see him. Now? I wish I never went, but I did. I was angry and planned to clear the air before Thorne brainwashed Camilla."

"About what?"

Luna exhaled a long, slow sigh. "Thorne twisted my arm until I let him adopt Sherlock. I wish I'd listened to my better judgment, but I'm such a sucker when it comes to my babies." She picked up two puppies and cuddled them close. It seemed like they gave her the strength to continue. "I need to back up."

I gestured for her to continue.

"The first time Thorne came here he was alone He showed sincere interest in the dogs and what I'm doing. He asked smart questions and complimented me. I'll admit that probably clouded my judgment, but I never got any weird vibe from him. He left and made an appointment to come back with his half-brother. He said they were both interested in adopting. It all seemed fine."

"Until he brought Gary on the next visit?" I asked.

"Sort of. The two of them shared a lot of looks, but I brushed it off as a brother thing." She shrugged. "Who am I to judge someone else's relationship?"

"Is that when Thorne showed an interest in Bones?"

"Yes, but not to the point where I thought he wanted to adopt him. That didn't come until the third visit.

"And he knew about the seizure disorder?" I asked.

"Of course. I was completely upfront about the dog's situation. It wasn't until I mentioned that I was keeping him that they started to show some interest." She handed Luke the two puppies in her arms. "Listen, how about we take this conversation into my house. Everyone, grab a puppy or two. I'll use your visit for some extra puppy socialization. They can never get too much."

I didn't hesitate. Two puppies were trying to climb up my legs, so I grabbed them, and Maggie scooped up the last two.

Luna double-checked that the pens were securely closed, then headed toward the door. "Follow me. Come on, Sasha. You get a special visit, too."

I couldn't complain about having puppies in my arms, but I did wonder if Luna was selling us a story that might not be true.

Chapter Fourteen

LUNA'S HOUSE WAS neat and cozy. "Make yourselves comfy," she said. "Thirsty? I'll be right back with some water."

One of the puppies in my arms started chewing on my hair while the other one sniffed my neck, tickling me and making me laugh. I plopped on the floor and gave them their freedom. Maggie and Luke did the same. We put our legs out, our feet touching in a makeshift circle, not that it stopped the puppies from trying to climb over us. Sasha leaned against me like she was a fifty-pound sack of dog food until I tapped the floor, and she stretched out. What a sweetheart.

"These puppies are adorable," Maggie said. "Can we take them all home? Maybe a sleepover with Bones and Pip?"

"Mags, these puppies are Luna's livelihood. I doubt they do sleepovers."

"Well, they should. It could be a new thing she offers."

Luke groaned. "I can see it now. Sea Breeze covered in wall-to-wall black Labradors with a sign that says twenty bucks for an hour of cuddles."

Luna returned with a water pitcher and glasses on a tray. She filled four glasses, handing one to each of us. "So, did I just hear that you want to pay me for puppy cuddles? Not a bad idea. I could use the income." She held up her glass in a toast to the idea.

"I'd pay," Maggie said. "But only if you let me take one home for a night or two. That's what you didn't hear, a puppy sleepover."

Luna practically spilled her water when she let out a big belly laugh. "That's a novel idea, and you know? I'm going to give it some thought. I have to do something to keep this business afloat. That's probably why I let Thorne talk me into his scheme."

The puppies crawled over our legs, but between the four of us, we managed to round them up and bring them back into our circle. I tucked one inside my jacket pocket, and it settled right down.

"Running a business creates all kinds of hurdles," Luke said. "My dad had someone who tried to swindle him out of our land. You can never be too careful."

Luna grimaced. "That's for sure. And now look at the mess I'm in—a suspect in a murder."

Maggie cuddled two puppies under her neck. "So, what happened?"

Luna looked off into the distance at nothing. I guess she needed to get her thoughts together or maybe decide how much she wanted to share. She barely knew us, after all.

She finally spoke. "Thorne and his brother convinced me they had plans to train Sherlock and Watson as therapy dogs. They told me they'd recently lost their mother, and a therapy dog had given her a lot of comfort toward the end of her life. I swallowed the story hook, line, and sinker."

"But?" I said, hoping to keep her talking.

"But it was all fake. I should have done background checks like I usually do *before* we all signed the contracts. But their story tugged at my heartstrings. I guess I'm a sucker that way."

Maggie stood up and paced. I could tell she was agitated. "Their mother didn't die. There was no therapy dog?"

"You guessed it. Once they had Sherlock and Watson, they threatened to expose Sherlock's medical condition unless I sold them the whole business! I refused, of course. It was ridiculous. I never hid the seizure disorder, but they planned to go to the papers and spread the lie that I ran an unscrupulous business. I'd have to fight them in court, and I don't have that kind of money. I went to the *Grapevine*, planning to talk to Cam so she heard my side of the story before she jumped on Thorne's bandwagon. But Luna and Thorne were in such a heated argument, I never got a chance to talk to her."

"Did they actually offer to buy your business for a fair price?"

Luna made a choking noise. "Hardly. They offered a pittance. Many of my puppies go to a seeing-eye program. I always have a few that don't qualify, like Sherlock, and then I look for good homes for a price that covers my expenses. Listen, I don't make a fortune with what I do, but I love it. I know I'm providing an important service. Thorne and his sleazy half-brother wanted to destroy all that."

I was flabbergasted, as were Luke and Maggie. I even noticed Maggie swipe a tear off her cheek. The story really got to her.

"You can see my predicament." Luna put down the two puppies that she'd been holding. With her arms waving around as she spoke, she looked a little unhinged. "I admit, I was at the scene of the crime, and sure, I definitely wanted Thorne and his half-brother out of my life because of the lies. But is that a motive to murder him? I can't hide from this, but I don't know what to do to defend myself."

I reached for Luna's arm, focused, and determined to be supportive. "Listen, Luna. I'm not going to sugarcoat any of this. You're in a difficult situation. But if you're innocent, the solution is to find the real killer. Maggie's a private investigator. Together, we're committed to finding Thorne's killer."

Maggie nodded. "That's right, to protect Bones. Maybe that's why he found me, so we can all help to solve this murder."

Luna looked dumbfounded for a moment, then her lower lip began to quiver until she couldn't hold in her emotion any longer. She dissolved in sobs. "I don't know what to say. Bones found the right person for him and for me because I'm innocent."

Luke stood up and stretched. "As adorable as these puppies are, I'm getting too stiff sitting on the floor. Luna? Can I ask you a question?"

She nodded but looked a little concerned.

"How did Thorne and his half-brother get along when they were here?"

"What do you mean?"

I was so glad Luke came with us. He was quiet but asked important questions that slipped my mind because I was too distracted by the puppies. Maybe that was Luna's plan.

"Well, you said Thorne came alone the first time. Were there any red flags?"

"Not at all. Now? Definitely. But isn't hindsight always when you see everything more clearly?

She had a point.

Luke continued. "When they were both here, who took the lead with the negotiations?"

Luna pursed her lips in thought. "Gary was much more aggressive, and Thorne did act uncomfortable with his behavior. You know, it was like a good guy-bad guy thing. Thorne was friendly and open, but Gary questioned everything I said and put me on the defensive."

"Who paid for Watson and Sherlock?" I asked.

"Thorne paid. He was definitely the money guy. Gary even hinted that Thorne had enough money to put me out of business whether or not I sold the business to them. He spun it like they were doing me a favor. Thorne didn't like that at all. And that's pretty much when everything broke down. Unfortunately, I'd already sold the two dogs to them. I'll never forgive myself for that."

Maggie patted Luna's shoulder. "I have Bones, and I'll give him the best home he could possibly have."

That didn't seem to reassure Luna very much or assuage the guilt eating at her. Time was the only cure for her poor judgment of Thorne and Gary.

Even though I wasn't a hundred percent sure she was innocent, I liked her and hoped she was. At any rate, I'd do anything to help her dogs. "I saw Gary on the beach this morning with Watson. To be honest, I don't think he's up for the responsibility. Maybe we can get Watson back for you."

"Really?" She totally perked up.

Maggie spun around as if a live wire shocked her. "If Gary murdered his brother to get control of Thorne's money, he won't be able to take Watson with him when he goes to jail. We have to figure this out, Dani, and save that poor dog."

It was exactly what I'd planned *not* to say. I didn't want to get Luna's hopes up. Too late for that.

"Can you help me bring the puppies back to the kennel before you leave?" Luna asked.

Who could say no to that request? Certainly not me. I scooped up the two I'd already snuggled and let them lick my cheek. At least, I think it was the same two, but it was hard to tell. Oh, my goodness. Pip was going to be jealous. First, I left her home, and second, she'd smell this puppy scent all over me.

I had plenty to think about. Not Maggie, though. She hummed as we drove away from Luna's Labradors. I could tell that she was full speed ahead to find Gary guilty of Thorne's murder and save Watson. The thing was, Gary had rubbed me the wrong way when we saw him on the beach, but Luna hadn't been particularly civil when she barged into the diner earlier.

I wasn't convinced about her.

Oh dear. It wasn't easy sorting out who had the means, motive, and opportunity. But for now, Camilla, Luna, Gary, and Lyndsey were all in the area, and all had varying degrees of motive.

Oh boy. What a mess.

Chapter Fifteen

MAGGIE DROVE STRAIGHT to Sea Breeze, chattering the whole way about how great Luna was and how lucky it was that she didn't insist on taking Bones away. I only half-listened until she said, "I'm sure Gary is the killer. One, Luna said he and Thorne didn't see eye to eye about starting a business. Two, it was all Thorne's money, so with him out of the way, Gary probably figures he'll get his hands on that lottery ticket one way or another. Three, I just don't like the guy."

"You haven't even met him, have you, Mags?" I asked, shocked that she'd been so easily swayed.

"Well, no, but you said you didn't like him."

When had my normally level-headed friend become so quick to jump to conclusions? And a private investigator to boot. Right after she seemed to have moved on from her irrational jealous streak over AJ, she'd verbally convicted Gary of murder when she barely knew him. This wasn't how anyone solved a murder. And it wasn't her normal level-headed thinking style.

"Maggie?" Luke said. "Take a step back. We know you don't want to lose Bones, but jumping to conclusions based on nothing isn't the best way to keep him in your life."

She looked at Luke. "Nothing? How can you say that? Didn't you listen to everything Luna said?"

"You can't believe everything before you dig deeper. That's your training," he argued.

I was glad that he sounded as annoyed as I felt.

I leaned forward, pushing my face close to Maggie's. "Luke's right, Mags. We all liked Luna and felt compassion for her story, but her information needs to be verified. What didn't she tell us? A good starting point would be to talk to her vet, don't you think?"

Maggie flicked her wrist dismissively and fiddled with the radio, a sure sign she was frustrated with my comment. "Yeah, yeah. I hear both of you loud and clear. But I listen to my gut. In the past, it has always steered me in the right direction." She looked up from the radio and focused on the road, speaking through clenched teeth to get her point across. "Listen. The picture I have of Gary Waite is someone who feels entitled to take what he wants by any means possible. So, he wants a business? No problem, he threatens the owner. He needs money? No problem, he uses his brother until that brother gets in his way. Then boom, dead. Mark my words, Dani. That guy is trouble."

I looked away from Mags to gather my thoughts about the brothers, taking in the boats on Blueberry Bay. But they couldn't offer enough of a distraction from the disturbing topic of murder.

I didn't disagree with Mag's point about the trouble part, but I wasn't blind to the possibility of someone else being the murderer. Sure, we liked Luna, but we liked Cam, too. And she had the best access to the murder scene through the staircase from her apartment. And I couldn't rule out the ex-girlfriend, Lyndsey. She was near the scene of the crime, and I reminded myself that she didn't shed a tear about Thorne's death. She seemed more interested in covering the story for the *Blueberry Bay Grapevine*. Maybe she thought she'd uncover information about the whereabouts of the lottery ticket and keep it for herself.

I faced Mags, well, the back of her head. "The point is, Mags, other people near the scene of the crime had a beef with Thorne. Don't lose sight of the big picture because you're so focused on Bones."

She screeched into my driveway and slammed on the brakes. At the sudden stop, I crashed into the back of the seat. "What the heck are you doing?"

She whipped her head around and glared at me. "Is that what you really think, Dani? That all I care about is Bones?"

"I didn't say that, and you know it, Mags."

"It sure sounded like it to me. This is what I think, Dani. You can stick your nose in everyone else's business but stay out of mine. Get out. Both of you."

I did, and so did Luke. I slammed the door shut and walked to my house without saying another word. What was the point? Maggie had lost all sight of who really cared about her, and I couldn't reason with her when she was in this dark place. She was worried about losing Bones. I got that. But the bigger issue, in my opinion, was the mess around AJ. And that was a relationship I couldn't be in the middle of.

Luke opened the door, gently put his hand on the small of my back, and we went inside. I didn't have to check the driveway. I knew Maggie had left from the squeal of her tires.

"She'll come around," Luke said. "She's scared. Her life is stuck, and she doesn't know which way it's headed."

"Yeah," I said, not at all convinced Luke was right.

For all I knew, Maggie might pack up and leave without saying goodbye. She could be impulsive like that. I bent down, and Pip flew into my open arms. Bones followed right behind but stopped short when he didn't see Maggie.

Luke chuckled. "She'll be back."

"Hey, Bones." I ruffled his ears. "Did you miss Mags?"

He sat, looked at me, and tilted his head. The door opened behind me.

"Dani? I'm sorry," Maggie sobbed. "I'm a bigger mess than I realized. I can't believe that I left without Bones. I'm not fit to take care of him."

He woofed and charged Maggie, knocking her against the wall. She slid down and let him lick her face, probably so we didn't see the tears.

"It's okay," I said and held out my hand. "Come on, let's make a plan."

"Okay. In a minute." She sounded miserable and it broke my heart.

Luke and I left her there, on the floor with Bones. She'd come to us when she was ready.

When we walked into the living room, Rose was just walking in from her apartment. "What was all the commotion about? I was worried there was an intruder."

I dismissed her concerns with a wave of my hand. "Just Bones making a racket when he was thrilled to see Maggie."

She chuckled and said, "Well, both dogs slept the whole time you were gone, so Maggie doesn't have to worry about leaving him with me if she needs to. It's been nice and quiet here until three minutes ago." Rose folded herself onto the couch, facing the view."

I felt a surge of joy that my family lived so close around me.

"What happened at Luna's?" Rose asked, oblivious just then to my moment of happiness that brightened our worry about the murder that had darkened our day.

I slid next to her on the couch and told her everything Luna shared with us.

Rose listened intently, the wheels in her agile brain turning before she said, "Luna had a lot to lose if Thorne convinced Camilla to print something negative about her dogs."

"True. But would she do that without checking into his allegations further? You wouldn't have printed something like that when you owned the *Grapevine*." I patted the couch, and Pip jumped next to me, her paws on my legs as she stared at me. I knew exactly what she wanted.

"How about a quick walk?" I asked her.

Pip yipped, jumped off the couch, and ran to the French doors.

I called to Maggie in the other room. "Mags? We're taking Pip down to the beach. Want to come?"

She walked in with Bones at her side. His tongue hung out, his tail wagged like a flag in the wind, but Maggie still looked distraught.

"Dani? I can't believe I said that stuff to you. I *do* want you to butt into my life. You tell me like it is, and I need that check on my impulses. Next time, knock some sense into me. Okay?"

I laughed. "My pleasure, Mags. As long as you promise not to pull your gun on me."

She smiled. The twinkle returned to her eyes. "Bones and I are ready for that walk now. But a quick one because I want to introduce him to Radar. I can't put that off forever."

The dogs raced to the beach ahead of us. The tide was out, luring lots of seagulls to land on the sand, searching for tidbits. Pip and Bones were in doggy heaven, chasing one bird only to have three more tease them. The wind whipped my curls around my face, and I pulled my fleece tight. We walked in a pleasant silence, almost to the lighthouse path, before we turned back. No one else was on the beach, making for a perfect walk as far as I was concerned.

Pip led the way up the stairs to our patio, with Bones jogging right behind.

"Those two are best buddies, don't you think, Dani?"

"Absolutely. Just like we are, Mags. Don't worry about what I said before. If we can't argue and forgive each other, our friendship is meaningless. We'll never agree on everything, but that's okay. I need your perspective."

"And I need your patience and wisdom." She sighed. "I'll just have to accept that I have no filter and blurt out every old thing that pops into my head."

"What a team," I said, and meant it.

When we walked inside, I felt so much better until I looked at Rose.

"Detective Winter was here," she said. "She wants Maggie to bring Bones to the police station. Luna brought in her contract and insisted she return him to her."

Maggie's jaw dropped. "That lying toad. I can't believe she completely deceived me."

"You have to call AJ," I said. "He told me it was his decision about Bones. Don't let Winter railroad you."

"Are you kidding me? No one railroads Maggie Marshall and lives to talk about it."

Fire burned in her eyes. She'd fight for Bones with everything she had, even if it meant calling AJ.

Chapter Sixteen

WITHOUT A SECOND thought, Maggie pulled out her phone and turned away from us. She didn't leave the living room, so I suspected she wanted our moral support, even if she pretended to need privacy.

"AJ? Maggie. I'm keeping Bones. Don't even argue about it."

I couldn't hear AJ's reply, but Maggie's head bobbed up and down. Was that a good sign?

"Okay. Good. Thank you," she said. "Sure, see you later."

She slid the phone back into her pocket and faced us with a big grin. "He's taking care of the problem. He said he wasn't aware of Luna contacting Jane, and since he's the lead on this investigation, he makes the rules. Great, right?"

"Right," I said, knowing there was more.

"And he asked me to meet him for dinner at the Blue Moon Inn tonight at six." Somehow, her grin grew even bigger. "I'm going home to get ready."

"It's only four o'clock, Mags," I said. How long did it take her to get ready for a date? Obviously, longer than I'd need.

"What's your point? I'd better hurry. I need time to get Bones settled in with Radar, and I have to look my best. I plan to knock the socks right off that guy, so he never even thinks about Jane Winter. Ever. Come on, Bones."

"Maggie?" Rose said before she disappeared with her love-struck expression. "Drop Bones off here with me when you leave for the Inn. It's probably better he's not alone, don't you think?"

Maggie's eyes popped wide. "Do you think that witch Luna might try to steal him?"

I wouldn't put it past her, but I kept my mouth shut, knowing Rose would handle the situation.

"Better safe than sorry."

"Right. I'll swing by and drop him off. Thanks, Rose."

After Maggie and Bones left, the house settled into its normal quiet mode. The clock ticked, and waves crashed below as the tide came back in. I kicked my shoes off, ready to relax on the couch until dinner.

I felt Luke staring at me as if he had something to spill. "What?"

"Dani? Don't get too comfy. I made reservations for dinner tonight. At six. At the Blue Moon Inn. Lily's making something extra special."

I dropped my head until it rested on the back of the couch. "Can we sneak in without letting Maggie and AJ know?"

"Actually, I suggested to AJ that he and Maggie join us." He held his hands up defensively. "Before you say anything, hear me out. When I talked to AJ earlier today, he was distraught. You know they're going through a rough patch, and he needed help putting their relationship back on track. Since she's one of your best friends, having dinner together seemed like a good idea."

I didn't know what to say. Did I want to spend my birthday dinner with Maggie and AJ? Not really, but Luke looked at me with such compassion, I couldn't help but love him for understanding what my friend needed, even when I preferred to ignore it and hope for a break. I stood up. When I got close, he wrapped me in his arms. I leaned my cheek against his strong chest and let his calmness surround me.

"That's exactly what Maggie needs. Does she know the plan?"

Luke shrugged. "I'm not sure. But I'm pretty sure AJ made a decision about their future."

"And?"

"Again, not sure, but don't you think she'll need us there to help celebrate if he pops the question?"

"Luke, I hope that's the plan and not that he wants

us there to pick up the pieces after he lets her down gently."

"Let's hope it doesn't go in that direction."

Rose, always the one with sound advice, said, "If you want my two cents, those two are madly in love. Once they get out of their own way, their passion will guide them. Will it still be rocky? Of course. It's who they are, but they'll make it work."

I wished I had Rose's confidence.

She stood up slowly as if her seventy-three years were finally catching up to her. She walked to the window. "This view never gets old. Just like two people when they figure out how to blend their strengths and weaknesses together. Like you two. This dinner plan is a great idea. You're the best role models for Maggie and AJ. Now, I'm going back to my apartment to find something for dinner. Come on, Pip. It's you and me tonight, watching the stars pop out over Blueberry Bay."

Before she left, I hugged my grandmother. "Thank you."

"For what? Speaking my mind?"

I stepped back. "That, and for being the smartest, kindest person I know. Although, it's a close tie with Luke. You two keep me grounded when I lose sight of what's important—Maggie, for one, making sure Bones stays with her, and figuring out who killed Thorne Waite."

"All in a day's work, Dani," Rose said and chuckled. "Say hello to Lily. She prepared a gastronomical miracle for you tonight. I know because she ran the menu by me to be sure you'd approve. You can tell me all about this date tomorrow."

"You knew all about this?"

"Well, yes. Don't look so shocked, dear. Luke wanted your dinner at the inn to be perfect. Of course, he never factored in a murder or AJ and Maggie's messy relationship. But that's life. Turning those lemons into sweet lemonade is your superpower."

I'd never looked at it that way.

"I'll see you two tomorrow. Come along, Pip. We have big decisions to make—grilled cheese or a BLT for me and chicken or ground beef for you."

Pip yapped and followed Rose without even a glance back at me. Traitor.

Luke draped his arm over my shoulders. "She's right, you know. You do have a superpower to make things right in the world around us. We all help, but you keep the end game in focus."

He spun me around to face him. "Happy Birthday, Dani. It's not exactly the day I had planned, but maybe we'll end on a high note at the Blue Moon Inn without more drama."

I laughed. "With AJ and Maggie at our table? There will be drama. You can count on it."

"True, but that's what makes them who they are. Did you notice something, Dani?"

I looked around the living room, half expecting to see a new side table he'd made or a new piece of artwork from a local artist. Nothing new. "Maybe I'm too distracted, but I don't see anything."

Luke led me to my favorite chair that faced Blueberry Bay and gently pushed me down. "Wait here," he said.

What had I missed? Our beautiful home was exactly how I'd left it in the morning. Except for one important item—Luke. I smiled. I couldn't be more perfect.

He returned with two glasses of wine and a plate with cheese and apple slices. "Your favorite—crisp blueberry wine." He gave me a glass then sat in the matching chair on the other side of our coffee table.

I noticed something else in his hand. He handed me an envelope.

"What's this?"

His eyes twinkled. "Take a look, Dani." Luke sipped his wine.

I slid out a card covered with a beautiful garden and the words FOR YOU. I opened it. Inside was a gift certificate for a weekend away, including two nights at a bed and breakfast near the Coastal Maine Botanical Garden.

"This is perfect, Luke!"

"We can go next month or next spring. Your choice."

"I couldn't be happier. A getaway to look forward to, and now sitting here, just the two of us."

"At least until we get to the Blue Moon Inn." He clinked his glass against mine. "To your birthday. If nothing else, it will be memorable."

That was an understatement.

The question was, memorable good or memorable bad?

Time was the only answer to that question.

Chapter Seventeen

THE BLUE MOON Inn, Lily's pride and joy, wrapped me in its quiet ambiance when we walked inside. Monday was typically the slowest night, but still, even though it was quieter than usual, more than half the seats were occupied. The inn itself offered six suites in the historic building, each uniquely decorated with antiques and deluxe appointments. The dining area, with flickering candles and strings of fairy lights, accommodated a dozen tables arranged so each had some privacy.

In my silky, dark-blue sheath, heels, and with my curls pulled into a twist, I felt like a princess.

Soft harp music filled the air accompanying the soft laughter and the tinkling of silverware on porcelain.

Luke gave his name to the hostess, and she showed us to a table in the back corner, secluded from other diners.

"There you are!" Maggie said, obviously elated when she saw us.

She jumped out of her chair, knocking it back. The crash made other diners look in our direction, but

Maggie laughed. I was glad to see her so happy. AJ stood up and smacked Luke on the arm in a typical guy greeting.

Then, he pulled out a chair for me. "For the birthday girl," he said and kissed my cheek.

I caught Luke's eye, and he winked as if to indicate this was all going in the right direction. We'd see about that.

"Dani? AJ and I got you a little something for your birthday." Maggie handed me a wrapped box. "Open it."

"How about champagne first?" Luke said.

"What a nice surprise this is," I said, settling my purse and wrap on the back of my chair. I put the box next to my place setting. "Tell me, Mags, how did you get here before us? I thought you were planning to bring Bones back to Sea Breeze to stay with Rose?"

She waved off my question. "Bones and Radar got along perfectly, so I left them together. They'll be fine. And listen to this. AJ straightened everything out with Bones, much to Luna's disappointment, I imagine. Can you believe what a crock of bird poop she gave us when we were there today? I'm happy he's with you, blah, blah, and more blah. Then she turns around and goes to the police. What a fraud."

"You went to Luna's today?" AJ asked in his deep detective tone. "You didn't tell me that, Maggie. Did you threaten her with a shootout or something equally intimidating?"

Maggie laughed a loud outburst from deep in her belly. It was obvious she was feeling no pain at the moment. "I wish I had, but no. She was super friendly. Letting us cuddle with the puppies and told us all about Gary and Thorne's supposedly devious plan to cheat her out of her business."

I held my hands up. "How about we don't discuss this tonight, Mags? Today has been drama on top of spectacle. I'd like to just enjoy the evening with all of you."

Luke covered my hand with his. "Dani's right. And here comes Lily with our champagne."

The bottle of champagne Lily carried looked like a cocoon wrapped as it was in a towel, but she also wore a worried expression. She handed the bottle over to Luke, tasking him to pop the cork.

She tucked a few stray hairs behind her ear. "Dani, I'm so glad you're here. I have a problem."

I caught her hand in mine. "What's wrong?" I knew how much the inn meant to her. Any problem caused her tremendous anxiety.

She glanced around as if checking to be sure no one was close enough to eavesdrop. "It's that half-brother who's staying here."

"Gary Waite?" I mouthed silently.

Luke, Maggie, and AJ stopped their conversation to

focus their attention on Lily.

"Yes. Gary and his dog, Watson. The problem is that Gary came back this morning after a walk on the beach, and a while later, that girl who works at Creative Design—"

"Lyndsey," I said.

"Yeah. Anyway, she came here looking for him, all agitated. Then, they both left without Watson. He's been locked in Gary's suite for several hours, and now he's barking up a storm. Not constantly, but I'm afraid it will get worse. My policy is that owners cannot leave their dogs unaccompanied at the inn. When they leave, they must take their dogs with them. But considering Gary's situation with his half-brother, I overlooked our policy when he left. I assumed he'd be back shortly, but it's been hours. I have to get the dog out of the room. Will you help me?"

Poor Lily had a dining room of guests to feed. I squeezed her hand, hoping it gave her some reassurance. "Of course."

Maggie put her hands on the table and stood up. She muttered through clenched teeth, "I'm coming, too. That dog needs a potty break, plus food and water. AJ? I'm taking him to my place to be with Bones. Let's go."

"But we didn't eat yet, Maggie. And I have a big surprise planned." AJ looked at me for support as if I could slow Maggie down. But, of course, no one could.

She patted his hand like she was soothing an upset child. "We'll come back, but don't you dare tell anyone where we're taking that dog. Understand? Anyone who abandons a dog for whatever reason doesn't deserve to keep him." She reached over and tugged on AJ's arm.

He looked at me, his raised eyebrows desperately expressing, *please intervene and talk sense into Maggie.* I shook my head no. In this case, I agreed one hundred percent with her. If AJ knew what was good for him, he'd get on board, too. And Watson sure wasn't going back to Luna.

In a desperate gesture, AJ took Maggie's hand and forced her to turn toward him. "Maggie, before you save the dog, I have to say something."

She rolled her eyes. "Make it quick, AJ. And don't you dare try to talk me out of this."

He dropped onto one knee.

Maggie's eyes popped open as big as saucers, and her hand flew to her mouth.

"Maggie? Will you marry me?"

It took about three seconds before she screeched and shouted, "Yes!" Then she pulled him into her arms, momentarily forgetting about Watson.

The diners nearby broke into applause.

Once they pulled out of their embrace, AJ said, "Maggie, this wasn't how I'd planned this moment. I planned to sneak the ring into your champagne, but what I love the best about you is the unexpected. You're on a mission to help Watson, and I'm all-in."

Luke slapped AJ's back. "For my two cents, well done. Dani and I will stay here, and you two can go with Lily to rescue Watson. You'll be back by the time the main course is served. Sound good?"

As much as I liked the idea of spending some time alone with Luke, this plan had problems as big as Blueberry Bay.

"Wait! Sit down for a minute. I have something to share, too."

Maggie and AJ reluctantly sat down. Luke popped the champagne cork and handed the bottle to Lily. She poured, and the other diners turned their focus back to their own meals.

Luke held up his glass. "To Maggie and AJ!" We clinked our glasses together.

Maggie leaned close to my ear. "Why are we wasting time, Dani?"

I leaned forward so only they could hear my quiet voice. "As an officer of the law, AJ has to stay away from going into that room, or he'll have to take Watson. So, here's what I propose. AJ leaves in his car with a work-related problem. Lily, give Maggie the room key. Mags, get Watson and go down the back stairs to your car. Be quiet and quick. Lily, when Gary comes back, tell him Watson slipped out when the maid went in with clean towels. He shouldn't have been in the room, and she was surprised when he ran out. Tell him you've contacted the police to help with the search."

Maggie kissed my cheek. "Brilliant."

AJ took out his phone. I heard him say something about a missing dog. He was jumping the gun a little, but who knew but us? He kissed Maggie and left.

Lily and Maggie walked casually out of the dining room.

I crossed my fingers. "What just happened?" I said, feeling completely drained. "Was this part of your birthday plan to get us alone?"

Luke's eyes twinkled from the flickering candlelight as he picked up his glass and tipped it in my direction. "Happy birthday, Dani. I couldn't have planned this if I'd tried. What now?"

We didn't have to wait long to find out what was next. Sue Ellen appeared wearing a frilly white apron and a huge grin. She carried a tray which looked so out of place I didn't know what to think.

"For the birthday girl."

"You're working for Lily now?" I was dumbfounded. Sue Ellen had more money than I could imagine and certainly didn't need a job.

"Just for tonight, honeybun. I'm your personal server. Your wish is my command."

I wished I could start the day over without getting

pulled into a murder investigation. But since even Sue Ellen couldn't afford a time machine, I didn't waste my wish on useless objects. Instead, I wished that Maggie and Watson made a clean escape.

"What's on the tray, Sue Ellen?" Luke asked.

She glanced at it as if she'd forgotten her job. Her smile brightened, and she said, "Oh, right," Then she carefully placed a cup of soup in front of each of us, without spilling a drop I noted. Then a basket of rolls magically appeared between us.

"There you go. Now let me see if I can remember what Lily told me. The soup is, um, minestrone with dried tomato pesto, and she made rosemary ciabatta rolls especially for you, in a spinach Dijon dip. I sampled everything, and Lily's food is heavenly."

"Thank you," I said, expecting Sue Ellen to leave so we could dig in. Instead, she pulled out the chair next to me and made herself comfortable.

"What was all the commotion?" she whispered. "Lily didn't have time to fill me in."

Would I ever get some time alone with Luke today?

Chapter Eighteen

WITH SUE ELLEN staring at me, waiting for information, I helped myself to a roll, dabbed on some dip, and took a bite.

"Oh, my goodness, Luke. This is so tender and light. Try one."

Of course, I knew Lily was an amazing baker, but nonetheless, the delicious combination of flavors caught me by surprise.

Sue Ellen tapped her fingers on the table. "Can I have that glass of champagne?" she asked, eyeing the partly filled glass in front of her.

"Really? Aren't you working?" I took another bite of the roll.

"Seriously, Dani? Give me a break. You're acting like you're annoyed with me, but I'm only trying to help Lily tonight with your birthday dinner. You and I both know that waitressing isn't my strength. I guess she figured if I messed up serving you two tonight, you'd forgive me. But that glass of champagne is calling my name. I could really use some reinforcement."

Luke chuckled and handed her Maggie's unfinished glass of champagne. "Cheers, Sue Ellen. Maggie won't mind."

Sue Ellen sighed, sat back, and sipped the bubbly. "I'm really sorry to intrude on your birthday dinner but fill me in on Maggie and AJ's drama. Pretty please? Where did they go? Does it have something to do with that sleazeball half-brother? That's why I stayed here with Lily, you know. I didn't want her to deal with him alone."

How could I stay annoyed with Sue Ellen? She was one of the most helpful people I knew, even if her style was sometimes clumsy. It wasn't fair of me to take my frustration out on her for my disaster of a birthday. I couldn't blame Sue Ellen or anyone else except whoever murdered Thorne Waite. That was what set everything else into motion, and that was where I had to focus my attention.

"Sorry, Sue Ellen. Today has been tough. First, the early morning phone call that woke me from a deep sleep, then finding the dog in the road, and to cap it all off, the murder." I leaned close to her and whispered, "The sleazy half-brother went out and left his dog in his suite. I'm sure you know that's against Lily's policy. She overlooked it for as long as she could, but the poor thing needed to go outside. She asked us to help because he'd started barking and disturbing the other guests."

"I knew it. Maggie took him, didn't she?" Sue Ellen's eyes lit up. "I knew she was up to something when I saw her scoot up the stairs. Knowing her, she stole that pup, and you know what? I don't blame her." Sue Ellen laughed.

"Well, I wouldn't say she stole him exactly. Let's just say she's keeping him safe," I said, not exactly sure of Maggie's long-term plan. "Lily's story is that Watson ran out when the maid went in with clean towels. The dog wasn't supposed to be there unsupervised."

Sue Ellen grinned. "Well, I just found a useful part in this charade for myself. Who do you think that maid was?" She ticked an eyebrow up. "I was so devastated when that dog ran past me. I'd better tell Lily so we both have the same story, but don't worry, I'll be back with your next course."

Sue Ellen left with her hips swaying as she charged to the kitchen.

Luke shook his head. "Your friends have an uncanny way of working together. I'm impressed. For a last-minute plan, it just might work." He split the rest of the champagne between my glass and his.

I sipped my bubbly and savored the taste, then said, "Might? There's no wiggle room in this, Luke." I set my glass down and said emphatically, "It has to work. I hope Maggie realizes that she'll have to walk the dogs one at a time, so no one sees them together. They're identical, so she has a chance of fooling even the most discerning eye."

"You mean Luna?"

"Luna will definitely be a problem, but we'll figure it out. I'm glad we can count on AJ now, too, even though it puts him in a difficult situation." I took another taste of the champagne, enjoying the fizzy buzz. Even with all the interruptions, I was beginning to enjoy the dinner.

Luke, facing the entrance to the inn, whispered, "Don't turn around, but AJ's coming back."

He arrived just as Sue Ellen reached our table, balancing a tray with our next course. I held my breath that she didn't spill our food. AJ stopped, notebook ready, and asked, "Did either of you happen to see a black Labrador in the parking lot when you arrived?"

Sue Ellen very carefully set the tray down on a folding stand next to our table. She held AJ's arm and said, "Detective? It was all my fault."

AJ looked a little confused, but Sue Ellen continued. "I went to suite number five, the Ocean View Room, to bring in clean towels while the guest was out. Maybe an hour ago? Anyway, when I opened the door, much to my shock, a black dog tore right past me and disappeared down the stairs. Scared me half to death!"

AJ nodded as if he wasn't quite sure what she was talking about. In the next moment, understanding flashed on his face, and he busily jotted in his notebook. "You didn't try to catch him?" he said without looking up.

"Oh, my goodness, officer. That black blur shot right past me like a streaking panther. I was frozen in a state of shock, and the poor pup was gone before I had a chance to even think about what to do. Have you had any sightings? I hate to think about him all alone in the dark." She wrung her hands.

I had trouble not laughing at Sue Ellen's knee-deep sob story. Maybe she'd laid it on too thick. Good thing Detective Jane Winter wasn't here with AJ. She'd ask too many questions and get Sue Ellen all tied up in knots.

AJ stuck his notebook in his pocket and gave Sue Ellen a little informal bow. "Okay. Thank you, Sue Ellen. I'm sure we'll find him. Don't blame yourself. The bottom line is the owner shouldn't have left the dog unattended in the room. Fortunately, Lily notified me quickly." He looked past me to the plates of food. "So sorry I ran out on this wonderful dinner, Dani, but duty called. Maybe a rain check?"

"Definitely," Luke answered. "Once all this has settled down, Dani and I will give you and Maggie a special dinner at Sea Breeze."

AJ nodded. "You both are great friends. Thanks for that pep talk this morning, Dani. My job had distracted me from what was really important."

"Maggie?"

His smile radiated a spark of happiness, then he walked away.

I didn't wait for Sue Ellen to serve our salads. This waitressing gig was definitely not her forte, but as soon as I took one and gave the other to Luke, she seemed to remember her spiel.

"Your salads are fresh peach with crumbled feta and radicchio chiffonade with a light balsamic vinaigrette. Lily outdid herself for your meal tonight. Wait till I bring the main course."

"Don't hurry, Sue Ellen. We're hoping Maggie makes it back, even if AJ can't partake. He's got to put in his best effort to find the dog."

"A purebred black Labrador? I bet someone stole that pup. You know, I poked my head outside after he ran off and saw a van parked across the street."

"Really?"

She winked. "I'll tell AJ to look for that vehicle."

I looked at Luke and raised my eyebrows. "Was Sue Ellen an actress in another life?"

"That would explain the special talent we've witnessed here. And I mean that in a completely complimentary way. Even the waitressing part. She's doing just fine."

Just as I took a mouthful of salad, one of the other diners approached our table. She looked to be around forty with mousy hair and big glasses. I think I'd seen her before, but I couldn't place her.

"Sorry to interrupt, but I accidentally heard about the lost dog. When we arrived tonight, I saw that white van across the street, too. The one that the waitress mentioned? There was writing on the door, but at the time, I didn't give it a second thought, and I didn't read what it said." She scribbled her name on a napkin and handed it to me. "Anyway, I'm on my way out. Can you give this to that detective if you see him again? I'm terribly worried about that dog. I'm happy to help in any way possible."

I covered my mouth and swallowed before I choked on the radicchio. "Thank you. I'm sure Detective Crenshaw will find the dog."

"He's working on that murder, too. Isn't he?" Her eyes sparkled a little too much for my liking.

I nodded.

She shook her head. "Such a tragedy. I knew the guy. Thorne Waite. Not well, mind you, but I knew he recently went through a rough patch regarding a young lady friend. And now this. So sad. Well, enjoy your meal." She turned and walked away like she was still remembering details.

I looked at the name on the napkin, "Trudy Moore," I read. "I know her. I've seen her at the diner with Lyndsey."

Luke nodded thoughtfully. "Maybe that's how she knew about Thorne's breakup. Do you know her well enough to ask her for more details?"

I folded the napkin with her name and tucked it in my pocket. "Not really, but has that ever stopped me before?" I shared a knowing grin with Luke. "Besides, she was awfully eager to interrupt our meal to tell us about that white van. I wonder if there really was a white van or if it was the power of suggestion? Sue Ellen winked at me like she was making it up."

"Interesting. But, if there was a van, maybe it was Luna's. She has a white van with her logo on the door."

"Waiting for Bones? That doesn't make sense."

"No, waiting for Gary to come out with Watson. The thing is, he went out without his dog. If it was Luna, Maggie needs to be super careful."

"Here she comes."

Maggie gave a quick smile when she reached the table, but it didn't mask how tired and troubled she looked.

"I'm worried. I think someone is following me," she said.

Chapter Nineteen

I PATTED THE chair next to me. "Sit down, Mags. Glad you made it back so quickly. Tell us what happened while we wait for Sue Ellen to bring out the main course."

"Sue Ellen?"

"Long story."

Maggie waved away any explanation. She reached across the table to AJ's empty spot and took his half-filled glass of champagne, downing it in one gulp. Then, she plucked a roll from the basket, something for her empty stomach.

Luke raised his finger. The closest waitress nodded and walked to our table.

"Can I help you? I can get Sue Ellen if you need something."

He glanced quickly at the wine list. "A bottle of chardonnay, please."

"I'll send Sue Ellen out with it, sir," she said and left.

Maggie sighed. "I've been running on adrenaline ever

since I let Watson out of that room. He's not very well-behaved. Certainly nothing like Bones. He stays glued to my side. But we made it to my place, and the two dogs were out-of-this-world happy to see each other. I left them together, closed in my bedroom. I think they'll be fine."

I stood up. "Mags? I want to hear your story, but first, the ladies' room. Wait until I get back to finish, okay?"

"Sure but hurry up. I don't plan to stay for long. I came back to ask Lily to bag up dinner for AJ and me."

"Good idea," I said and squeezed her shoulder. At best, this had to be incredibly stressful for her and dangerous at worst if, in fact, someone really was following her. But I knew Maggie. She'd put on blinders about any possible danger, thinking she could outsmart anyone else.

I walked past a couple of tables with couples deep in their private conversation, smiling and relaxed. I couldn't help but think about how different peoples' experiences could be under one roof.

The ladies' room, decorated with fresh flowers, antique framed mirrors, and individual dark-blue hand towels, created a relaxing ambiance. As soon as I entered though, I heard quiet sobbing coming from one of the two stalls. Should I say something? No. Instead, I quietly went into the other stall and gave the person time if she wanted to leave without bumping into me.

Once it was quiet, I flushed and walked out, only to see Lyndsey leaning against one of the sinks, her braids almost falling into the running water. She splashed some on her face. She startled when she straightened and saw my reflection in the mirror. I looked away, expecting her to leave.

Instead, she said, "I didn't hear anyone come in." Not that she needed to explain anything to me.

"Are you okay?" I handed her a fluffy hand towel, which I hoped she took as a friendly gesture.

"Not really. I wanted to impress Camilla with an article about Luna's Labradors, so I drove there with my notebook and pen, ready to do my first big interview. What a mistake that was. When I showed up, Luna said I was trespassing. She even threatened to call the police. I was scared. She acted kind of crazy if you ask me."

"What about your job at Creative Design?"

She flicked her wrist dismissively. "When Kelly got in, we had an argument, and I quit. I guess you could say this hasn't exactly been my best day."

"I'm so sorry. Do you have savings to live on?" I couldn't imagine being so impulsive unless she had a plan.

"I still have my yoga classes. That'll keep me from starving."

I washed my hands. "I went to Luna's today, too.

What time did you go?"

"A few hours ago, I guess. Gary called me out of the blue. Said he was lonely, so I met him here. He's far from one of my favorite people, but I needed to talk to someone who knew Thorne. We had that in common." When she shook her head, her long braids whipped around her face, almost as if she was punishing herself with a mild lashing. "Man, today has been one roller coaster of a ride. You know what I mean?"

I did, but I was sure the two of us were on different roller coasters.

"Can I ask you a question, Lyndsey?"

"Sure. I'm pretty much an open book." She looked at me with her big, innocent brown eyes, then threw the towel in the wicker hamper. "This sure is a fancy bathroom," she added, sounding impressed.

"Yeah, Lily's done a fantastic job with the inn. You know, she told me that you and Gary left here together. Did he go to Luna's with you?"

She leaned her butt against the sink and looked out the window. "He did. I told him I didn't think it was a good idea to come, but he insisted. I told him to stay in the car. The thing is, when Luna saw him, I think that's what set her off. She pointed at him in the passenger seat and screamed something about those brothers trying to steal her business. I don't know what she was talking about."

I helped myself to hand cream on the counter while Lyndsey applied lip gloss she took from her small bag. I spoke while she touched up her makeup.

"Why did Gary want to go? Did he bring his dog along? Was he thinking of returning Watson back to Luna?"

She stared at herself in the mirror, apparently satisfied with her face, then fiddled with the pendant on her beaded necklace. "When I met him outside, he didn't say anything about his dog. To be honest, I never gave it a second thought. Dogs aren't my thing. All he said was that he was lonely, and he didn't want to sit around in his suite."

Lyndsey inhaled like she was steeling herself for something challenging before she walked toward the door, ready or not, to face the world again. I sensed something still troubled her. Maybe losing her job or bungling her interview. I didn't know what, but something was on her mind.

"Before you leave, I'm wondering if you two talked about that lottery ticket you told me about. Gary told me he thought you had it."

She stopped and looked at me like she was completely baffled. "What? He told you that? What a sleazeball! That must be why he called me. I never considered he planned to throw me under the bus. He told me it was in a safe deposit box, just like I told you already. Why would he think I had it? I'm so done with him. He can hang out with his dog for company for all I care. Just like Thorne, always doting on that dog he got from Luna."

She pulled the door open. The force jangled her bracelets and made the door slam against the wall. Did I hit a nerve?

I approached our table, and Maggie gestured for me to hurry. She stood up as I came close. "I'm leaving, Dani. Lily boxed up two dinners, so AJ and I can eat together when he gets a break."

I hugged her and whispered. "Remember, you thought someone was following you, so be extra careful, Mags."

"Yeah, yeah, yeah. Don't worry. I know how to protect myself. You'll enjoy your romantic birthday dinner a lot more without me fussing and fidgeting next to you."

She had a point, but I'd still worry about her. I couldn't help it.

"Mags? Promise to text me when you get home and let me know everything is okay."

"I will," she said and strode out of the dining room on a mission with only one thought on her mind.

Luke stood up and held the chair for me, and I slid into it, then he sat next to me, taking my hand in his. "It's just the two of us, after all. Lily said the main course is on its way."

Even with all the drama, I realized I was hungry, especially for Lily's creation.

I reached for my wine. My hand bumped into Maggie's present. I picked up the box wrapped in gold paper. "Do you think Maggie will mind if I open this now?"

"I doubt it. Go right ahead."

I gave it a careful shake. Nothing rattled inside. I opened the card—a lovely scene of Blueberry Bay painted by a local artist and HAPPY BIRTHDAY, LOVE MAGGIE AND AJ written inside.

I looked at Luke. "Do you know what's in the box?"

He shook his head.

I pulled on the bow and let the red ribbon fall aside, then I carefully slid my fingernail under the tape instead of destroying the pretty paper. I opened the hinged box. Inside, nestled on soft cotton, was a solar-powered crystal. I held it up, marveling at the many facets that reflected every bit of light, even in the dim lighting here in the Inn.

"This is perfect! I'll hang it in the window facing the ocean so when the crystal revolves, it'll send rainbows around the room."

"It'll drive Pip crazy," Luke said. "He'll try to catch the moving light."

"Maybe."

My phone beeped with an incoming text message from Maggie. I put the crystal back in the box and picked up my phone. My blood ran cold when I read her message. *"Home. Dogs are gone."*

"What?" Luke said, taking the phone out of my hand.

Lily came to our table. "It will be a few more minutes, I hope you two are starving!" She must have seen the worry on my face. "Dani? What's wrong?"

"We have to leave right now," I said, but my legs didn't seem to work. "Maggie needs help. Someone broke into her house. The dogs are gone."

"Oh, no!" She wrapped me in a tight hug. "Go. Sue Ellen can bring your birthday dinner and dessert to Sea Breeze."

I finally managed to stand up without feeling wobbly. Lily hugged me again as if she was afraid to let me leave. "Be careful. I don't know what's going on today, but something's in the air."

She was right.

Luke put his arm around my waist, and we left what should have been a beautiful romantic evening.

When we arrived, I was giddy with anticipation.

Now?

The unknown had me scared out of my wits.

Chapter Twenty

IT WASN'T FAR from the Blue Moon Inn to Maggie's cottage, only a few miles before Sea Breeze, but it felt like we'd never get there. Every curve on the normally scenic drive slowed us down. The driver in front of us acted like he couldn't find the gas pedal.

I wanted to scream.

I tapped my foot impatiently and looked at my phone, hoping for more information from Maggie. "What happened to the dogs?" I asked as if the phone might magically answer me.

Of course, Luke had no more of a clue than I did and didn't bother to give an answer. He zipped by the slow driver as soon as he had a clear view.

Finally, we pulled into Maggie's driveway. Her cute cottage glowed as bright as a night carnival.

I ran inside.

"Mags?" I shouted.

She walked around the corner from her bedroom, looking worse than I'd ever seen her. Dark circles had settled beneath her eyes, and her shoulders sagged under the weight of her worry.

"What happened?"

"I shouldn't have left them here alone. While I was gone, someone broke in. When I got back from the inn, I found the back door wide open." She pointed to the door that led to her deck overlooking the beach and Blueberry Bay.

"And Radar?" I asked, worried that her inside kitty was gone, too.

"He's curled up on my pillow, as if nothing traumatic happened." She shrugged. "You know how cats can be. She was probably relieved to get her space back."

Maggie sank onto one of her living room chairs. "AJ told me to wait until he got here. Do you know how hard that is for me? But I can't have him worrying about me running around like a frantic beheaded chicken."

Luke put his hand on her shoulder. "He's right, Maggie. You need to wait here. AJ will do everything he can to find the dogs. Maybe Dani and I can help. We'll go down to the beach and look there. Who knows? Maybe they got away from whoever broke in when they opened the door."

Her head jerked up. "That's a great idea. Something I never considered because I only imagined the worst. I assumed Luna knew I'd left, and she broke in to steal Bones but hit the jackpot when she found Watson here, too. I might never see them again, Dani."

Before I could console her, AJ walked in, and Maggie ran into his arms.

"You have to find them, AJ."

He stroked her hair. "Shh. I will. I promise."

While he comforted Maggie, I grabbed her big flashlight from the kitchen counter and walked into the dark night with Luke at my side. The strong beam of light made it easier to navigate the steps leading to the beach. I slipped off my heels before risking a twisted ankle and making a complete disaster of the evening. Normally, this would feel like a romantic evening jaunt, but under the circumstances, I only felt dread.

"Do you really think the dogs got away?" I asked when we'd reached the bottom.

Luke took my hand in his. "It's possible," he answered. "Those dogs are just big puppies, and from what Maggie said, Watson doesn't have much in the way of training. Unless whoever broke into her house put leashes on them, there's a good chance Watson bolted for freedom with Bones right behind for the adventure."

I could imagine that scenario. "But wouldn't Luna know enough to put leashes on them?"

"What if it wasn't Luna? Remember that Gary and Thorne had plans for the two dogs?"

"If that's true."

"Sure, but assume, for the sake of this discussion, it

is. Maybe Gary decided he wanted the dogs after all. Even if it was just to sell them or blackmail Luna. Who knows what he's capable of?"

Those thoughts horrified me. "But Watson is his dog, and Bones belonged to Thorne. Couldn't he just say Bones belonged to him now that Thorne is dead instead of breaking in and stealing them?"

"Maybe, maybe not. There's still the problem with the contract Thorne signed, and Luna has already gone to the police to try and get Bones back. Gary may have decided it was easier to just take them and disappear. Maybe that was his plan all along. Get Thorne out of the way, steal the lottery ticket, and take the dogs."

"But Bones went missing, which is how Maggie got involved," I said, adding to the speculation. "You know what else I think? When I bumped into Lyndsey in the bathroom at the Blue Moon Inn, she told me that Gary insisted on going with her to Luna's. He told her he was lonely. I think he wanted to let Luna know he was around and wasn't afraid to show up at her business. He's not through with her yet."

We'd reached the stairs going up to Sea Breeze with no sign of a dog on the beach, or for that matter, any other living creature. I walked slowly up the stairs, feeling more dejected with each step. My curls a mess around my face after our unsuccessful hike. Finding the dogs was like looking for a lobster in the ocean without a lobster trap. But suddenly, I heard barking.

I quickened my pace. "That doesn't sound like Pip," I said and ran to the French doors. Inside were two goofy black Labradors on either side of my little Pip, barking and jumping and looking like they couldn't love life more. What a beautiful sight!

"What do we do now?" I asked Luke as I reached to open the door.

He stopped me. "Wait, or we'll lose them again." He cracked the door just enough so I could slip inside, and when the dogs followed me, Luke squeezed inside, too. I tossed my heels aside.

Rose sat on the couch with a self-satisfied grin on her face. "The dogs showed up about fifteen minutes ago, wet and happy. I guess Bones remembered the way. I already sent Maggie a message, so she'll be here soon. Pip here, let me know we had company, didn't you, you smart girl?"

At the sound of her name, Pip jumped on the couch and licked Rose's face. I tried to jump in front of the two Labs, but before I could stop them, they followed Pip and piled on top of Rose. She squealed but didn't sound upset. I grabbed the Labs by the scruff of their necks and pulled them off the couch.

"You two need to learn some manners," I scolded. "And I know who the perfect person is to teach them to you. As long as we can keep you both with Maggie."

That could be a battle I didn't want to think about at the moment.

"Well, you'll be happy to hear that I have a plan," Rose said with a satisfied grin.

"Perfect. I don't need to hear it right now, though. It sounds like someone just arrived, and I'm hoping it's our dinner. I'm starving."

Luke stood up just as Sue Ellen swept into the room carrying a huge, insulated bag. Even with it closed, the aroma made me swoon.

"Luke? Be a dear and get the rest from my car. My poor, aching feet need a break. I haven't spent so much time running back and forth filling water glasses and clearing tables since I was sixteen working at the local lunch dive."

I couldn't picture Sue Ellen ever waiting on anyone, but then again, I hadn't known her when she was sixteen.

She sagged onto the couch, stretched her feet out, and sighed the sigh of contentment. Pip rewarded her with a sneaky lick on her cheek. Bones and Watson danced around Sue Ellen, wanting in on the fun, too, until she dug treats out from her tote.

"Here you go, you naughty pups. You gave us all a scare, but at least you're safe and sound here. Now, take your bones and settle down."

Rose already had plates and silverware at the table by

the time Luke carried in the last bag.

"How many meals did Lily send?" he asked.

"You know Lily. She made plenty for you and Dani, plus more for anyone else who might pop in. You know how that always happens here. One visitor stops by, and before you know it, every friend is sitting at your table."

I didn't plan to wait for any uninvited guests. I got myself a plate and looked at all the food, wondering where to start.

"Oh," Sue Ellen said. "Lily reminded me to describe all the food as if I was serving you at the inn." She slowly stood up, walked to the table next to me, and held her hand out as if formally presenting the meal. "Here you have chicken piccata with grilled asparagus, new potatoes in herbed butter, and fresh applesauce slightly sweetened with local honey."

The aroma assaulted my senses and made my mouth water even before I heard the description.

"Shall I serve you, Dani?" Sue Ellen asked.

"I'd love that."

Without any complaint, she carefully plated up the food in an artistic display. "We eat with our eyes, nose, and mouth. Something I learned from my grandmother, and Lily approves of my sentiment," she said and handed me the plate. Immediately, she prepared another for Luke.

I couldn't wait to dig in, but the door opened, and

the dogs went wild, jumping on Maggie before I even sat down.

"Dani? You have to show AJ that letter you got from Thorne."

"Let her eat her dinner, Maggie," Luke said quickly before something flopped out of my mouth that I'd regret.

He knew I was hungry, frustrated, and reaching my limit of drama for the day, but Maggie had a point. AJ needed to know about the letter and lottery ticket. Something I'd relegated to my brain's back burner but couldn't put off forever.

"You're right, Mags. That ticket might work as the trap to catch a killer."

Chapter Twenty-One

"THE FOOD'S HOT," Rose said. "Dani will have to eat and talk."

Sue Ellen took another plate. "Lily sent over plenty, so dig in."

It didn't take long for everyone to help themselves. Luke sat at one end of our table, with Rose at the other end. Maggie and AJ snuggled close on one side, Sue Ellen and I sat opposite. Each dog found a comfy spot to crash. As I looked around, I realized how fortunate I was to be surrounded by my friends and family in the comfort of my beautiful home.

Even with a murder hanging over us.

As Maggie reached for her wine glass, her engagement ring sparkled in the overhead light. Sue Ellen's eyes opened wider than a seagull zeroing in on a peanut butter sandwich. She reached across the table and grabbed Maggie's hand.

"What is this?"

Maggie actually blushed, an unusual look for her.

"AJ proposed at the Blue Moon Inn."

"And no one told me?" Sue Ellen sent a hurt look my way.

I felt a stab of guilt, but considering the day I'd had, I pushed it aside and mumbled, "There was a lot going on."

Luke, always there to have my back, raised his glass, drawing Sue Ellen's glare away from me. "To AJ and Maggie."

AJ kissed his sweetheart, lingering while we hooted and cheered for the couple.

When they pulled apart, Maggie wiped a tear from her cheek. "Don't any of you dare mention you saw me cry. It'll ruin my tough-girl image."

I snorted. "Everyone knows you're as tough as cowhide, Mags. Probably tougher."

Lily's delectable meal only added to the festive atmosphere at my table. I enjoyed every morsel to the fullest, then pushed my chair back before I burst.

"I hope you left room for your birthday cake, Dani," Sue Ellen said. "That's the best part."

I groaned and patted my overfull stomach. "Not yet."

Rose pushed herself up from her chair. "Good. We can get down to business, then. Dani? Get Thorne's letter from the safe, and I'll explain my plan."

Nothing like jumping from a relaxing occasion

straight to full-speed ahead. But when Rose had a plan, she had a plan, and nothing would get in the way.

I reluctantly left the pleasant chatter in the dining room, but Rose surprised me by getting up from the table and walking in step with me. "I want you to know that Cam is coming over," she said.

I did a double take. "What? Why?"

"Trust me on this. She's part of my plan to keep Bones with Maggie and honor Thorne's request for the disposition of the lottery money."

"Of course, I trust you," I said with a touch of indignation. When had I not? "It's just a surprise because I thought we were done with drama for today."

She hugged me, then held me at arm's length. "I know it's a lot to have Cam come by tonight. Especially since it's your birthday. You're tired, and you're looking forward to relaxing with Luke. I get it. But we have to stay ahead of this, Dani. I learned when I ran the *Blueberry Bay Grapevine* that if you push the news, you control the narrative instead of playing defense. That's my goal."

Her words washed over me like a warm, comfy blanket, giving me a boost of energy just as someone knocked softly on the front door. Soft enough, I noted happily, that the dogs didn't hear.

"Camilla?" I said.

Rose nodded. "I'll let her in. You get the envelope."

I heard Rose welcoming Cam inside, and I wondered exactly what her plan entailed. I read Thorne's note again. I DON'T KNOW WHAT ELSE TO DO BUT LEAVE THIS WITH SOMEONE I BELIEVE IS ONE HUNDRED PERCENT TRUSTWORTHY. I'M AFRAID MY LIFE IS RUINED AND POSSIBLY IN DANGER BECAUSE OF THIS STUPID WINNING TICKET AND SOME INFORMATION I'VE DISCOVERED THAT I WANT TO TALK TO CAMILLA ABOUT. IF SOMETHING HAPPENS TO ME, PLEASE DONATE THE MONEY TO AN ORGANIZATION THAT HELP'S DOGS IN SOME WAY. I LEFT A PHOTOCOPY OF THE TICKET AND THESE INSTRUCTIONS IN MY SAFE DEPOSIT BOX, TOO. TW

It gave me chills to think he suspected his own death.

I joined the others to find Cam in the middle of the room with her back to me. No surprise seeing her short, purple-tinted silver hair, but the girl next to her caught me off guard. Long braids and turquoise shirt meant Lyndsey came along, too. Why?

While the dogs distracted the two newcomers with a thorough sniffing, I quickly slid the envelope under my heavy picture book of Maine's lighthouses. I preferred to leave it safely out of sight until I knew exactly what Cam and Lyndsey were up to.

"Take a seat." Rose indicated the two chairs opposite the couch.

Lyndsey brusquely pushed past the dogs and perched on a chair with her notebook and pen at the ready. Cam, on the other hand, crouched down and gushed over them. "What beautiful dogs. Are they why you asked me to come over?" she asked.

"The dogs are certainly part of the reason, Cam. Once everyone is comfortable, we'll get to it."

I sat on the couch, and Pip jumped up, wiggling herself between Luke and me. Bones and Watson leaped onto the end of the couch, managing to curl up together. It was a tight squeeze, but it worked. Sort of.

Rose perched on the edge of the window seat. "Lyndsey, how nice of you to join us, too," she said, sounding sincere.

I didn't agree, but Rose had an agenda. Who was I not to follow it?

Lyndsey smiled and scooched forward even closer to the edge of the chair, eyes shining. Her petite frame practically rested on air. "I'm working for Camilla now, and she suggested I come along to help her on the article about Thorne's murder. Get my feet wet, you know? Not literally, of course." She was the only one laughing at her joke. Awkward, but she continued unfazed. "I also want to learn everything I can from Cam and you, too, Ms. Mackenzie. You must have every trick up your sleeve from your years of putting out the *Grapevine*." She paused as if deciding whether to go on or not. Hesitantly, she said, "If you don't mind me asking, how do you gain the confidence of your interviewees? I didn't have much luck this morning with Luna."

Rose smiled. "Time, patience, and experience, my dear. Unfortunately, it's not something I can teach you. You either have it or you don't. Oh, you can become competent, I suppose, but gaining someone's trust is almost a magical gift."

I suspected Lyndsey didn't possess that gift in any shape or form. Not from what I'd seen, anyway. Her style was blunt, in your face, with zero finesse.

Her face crumpled. Cam nodded for her to continue. "Oh, well, I guess I have some work cut out for myself. Can I ask what you know about Luna's Labradors? She wouldn't talk to me. The thing is, Gary said she's involved with something shady. He also found a note from Thorne that said he had something to tell Cam. I think it was about Luna. A motive for her to silence him?"

Did that mean Gary got access to the safe deposit box? If that was the case, he also knew I had the lottery ticket. I glanced at my hiding spot, glad to see the envelope was still hidden from view.

During the conversation, Sue Ellen bustled about clearing the table. Maggie and AJ sat huddled together on the loveseat like two lovebirds, but Maggie suddenly jerked forward, ready to explode when Lyndsey mentioned Gary's name. Thankfully, AJ held her back.

"That's interesting. Did the note say anything else?"

Rose asked, revealing no hint of what she was really thinking.

Lyndsey smiled like she had us backed into a corner. "Yes. Thorne wrote that he gave Dani the lottery ticket for safe keeping. I need to warn you, Gary plans to fight this as far as necessary. He says he's the rightful heir." For emphasis, she crossed her arms over her chest and raised her eyebrows.

In my opinion, she looked like a spoiled teenager and not someone displaying a speck of intimidation.

"Is that so?" Rose said in her normal cool, calm, and collected demeanor. Her eyes, though, were as cold as Blueberry Bay in December. "You can let Gary know that my lawyer is verifying the authenticity of the original note. I'm of the opinion that Gary doesn't have a leg to stand on. As both you and Gary acknowledged, the lottery ticket belonged to Thorne. He could do whatever he wanted with it—cash it in, give it away, or even burn it. And that brings me to why I invited Camilla here in the first place."

I caught the edge in Rose's voice and loved how she dismissed Lyndsey so easily. My grandmother definitely held a magical talent for communication.

Cam, silent until now, said, "Is this conversation on the record for me to print in the *Blueberry Bay Grapevine*, Rose?"

"Absolutely, Camilla. I'm giving you an exclusive

story, along with a copy of the note Thorne gave Dani. I want everyone in the Blueberry Bay area to know that his winnings will help dogs, just as he requested. Dani plans to start a service dog training facility partnered with Luna's Labradors. Assuming Luna is on board and is willing to provide puppies, of course."

Lyndsey's jaw dropped. "That was Gary's plan. You're stealing his plan."

"Absolutely not," I said now that I understood Rose's strategy. "Luna told me *Thorne* wanted to start a service dog training facility. I'm only implementing what he wanted to do with his windfall. Gary doesn't have the money for it, and I won't be needing his help. Plus"—I held up my hand before Lyndsey interrupted—"the contract for these two beautiful Labradors you see in here stipulates that ownership returns to Luna in the event either Thorne or Gary can't provide the proper care."

"But—"

AJ stood up. "That's right. I took responsibility for Thorne's dog when he was found running loose on the road, almost getting hit. That, plus Thorne Waite's tragic death forced me to appoint a foster parent until all the details are worked out."

"But what about Gary's dog? Gary isn't dead. You can't just steal his dog," Lyndsey said.

Now, it was Maggie's turn to squash this argument. She pointed to Lyndsey, shrinking back into the chair.

"Gary lost any right to that dog when he abandoned him at the Blue Moon Inn. Yes, I said abandon, and I meant it. It's against the inn's policy to leave a dog unsupervised. When Watson escaped and got lost, Detective Crenshaw"—she smiled at AJ—"got involved and took responsibility for him. Gary should feel lucky that he hasn't been fined for animal cruelty."

Lyndsey looked like she wanted to hide under the couch with my dust bunnies.

"You know what I think, Lyndsey? You don't care about helping Cam with her article. You came here pretending you have a burning desire to learn about journalistic secrets and flesh out an article but your real goal? Searching for information about Thorne's missing lottery ticket. That's the real reason you came here tonight, isn't it? To do Gary's dirty work?" I stood next to Maggie, both of us towering over her. "He didn't dare show his face here, but you have no scruples, do you?" I turned toward Camilla and directed my glare at her. "I expected better from you. You both need to leave now."

"And don't let the door hit you on the way out," Maggie added.

Lyndsey stood up and stared at me with eyes blazing. "Gary doesn't care about that dog, and neither do I. He wants what's rightfully his, the lottery ticket. You haven't heard the last about this." She stormed out the front door, and I couldn't have been happier to see her backside.

Cam hung back, though. As soon as the door slammed closed, she looked at Rose. "You were right about Lyndsey. She only cares about that lottery ticket."

It was my turn to be stunned. "What? You two planned this?"

Rose chuckled. "I told you I had a plan, Dani. It wouldn't have worked if you had known I was setting Lyndsey up to get information. Thanks to Camilla, we now know exactly what she and Gary are up to."

"But we still don't know who killed Thorne," I said.

"Maybe Lyndsey and Gary worked together," Maggie said.

"Luna still has a shadow hanging over her, too," I said. "I wonder if she'd do anything to protect her business, even murder, if it meant getting her hands on that lottery ticket."

AJ glanced at Cam, who shrank under his gaze. His meaning was clear, even if he didn't say anything. The staircase from her apartment to her office and the murder scene still left her as a suspect.

Chapter Twenty-Two

SUE ELLEN CALLED us back to the dining room. "We can't leave before—ta-da—the birthday cake! Come over here, Dani. Make a wish and blow out the candles, all thirty of them."

She held up her phone to document my moment for posterity, so I sucked in a big lungful of air and blew. The candles went out. Then relit again. What the heck?

"Great, Sue Ellen. Now my wish won't come true."

"Oh dear, I didn't think about that when I bought these trick candles."

I laughed. "It's okay. My wish will come true or not, regardless of the candles. But someone needs to put them out before the wax ruins the frosting. That would be a crisis I can't handle tonight."

Luke quickly pulled out each candle and dropped them wick-first into a water glass. "There. Now we can have cake. The best part of a birthday in my opinion."

Sue Ellen held up her hand. "Not yet! First, I have to tell you what Lily made. This is her signature carrot cake with orange ginger filling and maple-sweetened cream cheese frosting. Lily let me sample a cupcake, so I can assure y'all, it's beyond delicious!"

Rose sliced the three-layer cake, and Maggie added a dollop of whipped cream on top. Could it be more decadent? Probably not, and after the first taste, I decided it couldn't be more delicious.

Between mouthfuls, I said. "Thank you everyone. This cake tops off a memorable birthday."

Luke whispered in my ear. "It's not over yet."

Chills ran up my spine even though I was dead tired.

"Dani?" AJ said. "I think I should take the note and lottery ticket for safekeeping. Lyndsey probably suspects you have it here, and I'd hate to think she and Gary might try to steal it. What do you think?"

I looked at Luke. He nodded.

"Okay," I said. "You can keep it safe until I'm ready to cash it in. Mags, what about Watson and Bones? Where will they stay?" I had to admit, I enjoyed their company.

Bones was right at Maggie's side, so I knew he'd be going with her, but Watson was snoring on the couch next to Pip.

"Keep Watson here with you, Dani, but Bones stays with me. My cottage isn't really big enough for both Labs plus Radar anyway."

Maggie gave me a big hug. "Happy birthday."

"Thanks for the crystal. I opened your gift at the inn but haven't hung it up yet. Although, I know the perfect spot."

I passed the envelope to AJ, and they left, hand in hand, with Bones bumping against Maggie's leg.

"I could never seem to find the right time to give this to you, Dani. Happy Birthday." Sue Ellen held a present toward me. "Go ahead. Open it before I leave."

I carried the gift to the couch and sat down. Luke sat next to me as I carefully unwrapped the box. I glanced at Sue Ellen, sitting across from me with her hands held together at her chest. I think she was more excited than I was. Of course, Sue Ellen was an awesome gift-giver, so I was dying of curiosity.

I gasped. "Where did you find it?" I said, lifting a gorgeous double silver hair clip from the box. "Look, Luke," I exclaimed, pointing to the beautiful turquoise jewels adorning the clip. I pushed the wrapping to the floor and twisted my unruly auburn curls into a bun and held it together with the clip.

I turned my head one way, then the other. "How does it look?"

"Beautiful," she said, full of pride at picking the perfect gift. "It will be ideal to wear at Maggie and AJ's wedding. Do they have a date?"

I laughed. "No clue, Sue Ellen. But my guess is sooner rather than later."

Rose walked over with her gift for me. This day was ending on a high note, after all.

She had tears in her eyes when she said, "For you, Dani."

I didn't even know what it was yet, but I got choked up. I untied the ribbon and tore through the paper. Inside was a hardcover book, a little worn around the edges but still in great condition.

"*The Tale of Peter Rabbit*, one of my favorite books of all time. This first edition, inscribed by Beatrix Potter herself, belongs on your shelf now, Danielle." Rose said, her voice filled with emotion.

I didn't know what to say, so I pulled my grandmother into a tight hug and whispered, "Thank you. It's perfect. My favorite that you always read to me."

When she released me, she said, "Now, it's time for me to retire to my apartment and give you two kids some privacy. Besides, Trouble is probably lonely and wondering where I've been. But, before I go, promise me that you'll lock your doors. I'm convinced someone wants that lottery ticket enough to break in to steal it, even if it's not here. At least Pip and Watson will raise the dead with their barking. Sometimes, that's enough to scare off an intruder."

"Don't worry, Rose," Luke said. "We'll be safe tonight. My guess is that a thief will wait until the house is empty."

"Maybe, but it's best to be prepared."

With another round of hugs, Rose walked to her apartment, and Luke walked Sue Ellen to her car. When he returned, he double-checked that everything was locked up tight. Then we sat on the couch. I sighed. Outside, the stars twinkled over Blueberry Bay, the waves crashed on the beach, and the wind made the branches creak and sway. I was glad to be inside.

We sat quietly for several minutes.

"I know you want to talk about everything that happened today. That's how you process stuff, so spit it out, Dani."

Luke knew me well.

"You're right. Now that it's quiet, my brain is working through everything."

"And?"

"And I don't think Camilla killed Thorne. I just don't see a motive unless it was in self-defense, but wouldn't she own up to something like that?"

"You would think so, but people panic. We'll put her at the bottom of the list."

"Okay, that leaves Luna, Gary, and Lyndsey, right?"

"Right."

Watson lifted his head and growled. The hairs rose on my arms. I looked out into the dark night "What is it, Watson? Check the doors again, Luke. Just to be sure."

He silently padded across the wood floor with Watson following.

I texted Maggie. *"Is AJ with you?"*

She texted right back. *"Yes. Everything OK?"*

"Not sure," I responded.

"On our way," she wrote.

"Everything's locked up tight, Dani. But Watson is still restless."

"AJ and Maggie are coming over. It's probably nothing, just a new place for Watson that he's not used to, you know?" I was trying to convince myself that was the case.

"I know, but it's creepy."

I jumped up when I saw headlights flash through the window next to the front door. "They're here."

Maggie came straight to the door with Bones, and I pulled her inside.

"We saw a car parked on the road, but it pulled away when we got here, Dani. Unfortunately, we didn't get the license plate. AJ's walking around outside, checking everything. Now, tell me exactly what happened." Maggie said, taking my hand in hers.

"Nothing, really. Watson got restless and growled. I don't know if it's because it's a new place for him or if he actually sensed something. Honestly? It felt weird to Luke and me, too, Mags. Like a scary vibe in the air."

"Don't worry." Maggie put her arm around me, and we walked to the living room. "AJ will figure it out." She sounded relaxed, but they came so quickly; they must have been on high alert, too.

"Thanks for coming, Mags."

"Of course, and we're staying in your guest room tonight. Don't argue with me, Dani. We're here, and we're staying. Just to be on the safe side."

Was it overkill? Maybe, but I liked the idea.

AJ tapped on the French door, and Luke let him in.

"I didn't see anything out of place, but that car we saw drove off in a big hurry. It makes me suspect someone was sneaking around outside. Maggie and I will stay here tonight in case something else happens."

"Sure. The guest room is all set. You know the way, Mags."

"We all need sleep, so we'll talk more in the morning," AJ said.

That sounded good to me.

Everything would look better after a good night's sleep. At least, that was what I hoped.

Chapter Twenty-Three

MORNING CAME MUCH too quickly as far as I was concerned. When I rolled over, Luke's side of the bed was empty. Well, not exactly, because Pip had squirmed her way under the blanket near the top of the bed. Watson was curled up by my feet. It hadn't taken him long to make himself feel right at home.

I stretched and yawned, and then all the drama from the day before crashed down on me. Sliding out from under the warm blankets, I padded to my closet for a warm robe and slippers.

"Come on, you two lazybones. If I have to get up, you do, too."

Watson bounded off the bed in one leap, ready to charge into the day, full-speed ahead. Pip on the other hand, wiggled out from under the covers and carefully jumped off the bed. They greeted each other with tails wagging before Pip led the way through the partially opened door straight to the delicious aromas in the kitchen.

My kitchen was always the place to be in the morning. Depending on the day, coffee, tea, and usually blueberry muffins from the diner, waited for anyone who showed up hungry. At least when Luke got up first. Today, sunshine streamed in through the east-facing windows, a lucky omen as far as I was concerned since fog often shrouded us until midmorning.

Luke handed me a mug. I inhaled the peppermint aroma and kissed his cheek. "You got up early," I said and sipped the tea.

"I called Chad and Christy at the diner to let them know you'd be late, Dani. I hope you don't mind. Chad said they were fine."

Right. The diner. How could I forget my business? It usually took up all my brain bandwidth. "Thanks. I'm so lucky with those two. Any sign of Maggie or AJ yet?"

"AJ was up at the crack of dawn. Said he had to run back to the cottage for something. I don't know why he's not back yet. I guess something came up. Anyway, I imagine Maggie will be down soon."

I hung the solar-powered crystal in the window where it spun around and threw rainbows around the kitchen. The cheerful colors made me think I'd imagined the creepiness of the night before.

"Last night was probably nothing. What do you think, Luke?"

He sat down next to me with his coffee. "I don't

think it was nothing, Dani. Remember, Thorne gave you a lottery ticket worth a million dollars. I can understand how Gary thinks he deserves it, even if I don't agree. It was Thorne's ticket to do with whatever he wanted, and in my opinion, he made the right choice when he left it for you."

I elbowed him and laughed. "Yeah, no bias in that statement, is there?"

He held up his thumb and finger a quarter inch apart. "Maybe a pinch? But seriously, Dani. You don't plan to cash it in and ignore Thorne's request. You'll do right by his memory."

We sat, shoulder to shoulder, enjoying the peace and quiet, thinking about the heavy responsibility Thorne dropped in my lap. Quiet surrounded us until a dog clattered down the stairs.

"Slow down, Bones. You're gonna break your neck!"

Bones came to a sliding stop when he crashed into the kitchen island. He yelped but recovered once Watson ran in, and the two Labs were off. They chased each other through the house, but poor Pip barely made it onto the couch, escaping getting trampled in seconds. It was a lot of puppy energy, something they needed to take outside.

"Well, that's quite the good morning to you all, isn't it?" Maggie finger-combed her short hair, still tussled from sleep, and quickly had it in order. Next, she helped herself to coffee.

After a big sip, she said, "No one in their right mind would try to break into this house. By the way, any idea where AJ went off to already? I slept like the dead. I didn't even wake up when he snuck out."

I shrugged and said, "Text him, Mags. All he told Luke was that he needed to check something at your cottage."

I finished my tea and stood up to leave. "Who's coming for a walk on the beach. These dogs need to get outside."

Maggie, head down, busy texting, didn't answer, but Luke said, "I'll wait outside with the dogs while you throw on some clothes. But hurry. I don't think Watson and Bones will wait for long."

"Oh, no," Maggie said as she looked at her phone.

I leaned over to see the message, concerned. "What?"

She waved me off. "Take your walk. It can wait. Do you mind if I leave Bones here with you? I need to go to my cottage for a minute."

I watched her leave and wondered what that was all about but didn't have time to worry. I ran to my room and pulled on jeans and a T-shirt, and grabbed a flannel shirt, knowing the morning breeze could be chilly even in mid-August. When I opened the French door to the patio, the dogs were already chasing each other in a wild game of zoomies.

I stood at the top of the stairs, finishing my tea, the dogs anxious to dash onto the beach. "Pip, let the boys go first, or you'll get knocked head over paws."

She hung back, letting Watson and Bones fly down the stairs as if their feet had wings. How could I harness some of that energy for myself? Pip followed at a more respectable pace, but once on the beach, she took charge, chasing the waves and sprinting after seagulls with the two Labs right at her heels.

Luke took my hand. "Let's not go too far," I said. "The dogs can run here, close to home. I don't want to risk bumping into anyone."

Like Gary or Lyndsey, I left unsaid.

We sat on the sand, watching the dogs. Where was this drama headed? Could we save the two Labs plus figure out who killed Thorne? Was it for the lottery money or something else? Was there a connection between Luna's black Labradors, money, and the threat of a scandal?

I turned to Luke. "Don't you think it was odd the way Maggie left so suddenly? And without Bones," I said, breaking our silence.

Luke shielded his eyes from the bright sun, and from the way he raised his brows, I knew he agreed. That was enough for me. "Let's go back to the house."

Luke pulled me to my feet, and I brushed the sand from my jeans.

"You're right, it was strange. And AJ seemed distracted when he left."

He whistled and the dogs came running. "Let's go. First one back to the house gets an extra treat."

"Seriously, Luke? Pip's the only one who knows that word."

"And she deserves an extra something for putting up with the wild pups, right?"

I couldn't disagree. Pip made it halfway up the stairs before the two Labs realized where she was headed, so she won the race without even breaking into a pant.

Rose, in her slacks and a button-down shirt, looked ready for the day when Luke and I straggled into the kitchen after the dogs.

"Dani, it's busy at the diner. Do you want me to help today?"

"Absolutely. If you don't mind. I'll check in first and see if they're having any problems, but I suppose I should talk to Luna and let her know about the dog training idea." I chuckled. "She and her pups are an integral part of the program."

"Perfect. I'll go in with you then," Rose said and tied a new bandana around Pip's neck. I didn't know where she got her endless supply, but this one was gorgeous. Brilliant blue with pink hearts.

"What about Watson and Bones? Are they staying here today?" Luke asked.

He'd already rinsed the used mugs and placed two bowls of dog food on the floor.

"I'll keep an eye on the two wild pups. But you should take Pip with you, Dani. She knows your routine and might be happier without the Labs constantly bugging her. You can feed her in your office at the diner." He handed me a covered bowl with Pip's food.

"Good idea." I grabbed my bag. "Ready to go, Rose?"

She tied a scarf around her neck, a sure sign she was all set. We walked outside, and Pip made a beeline straight to my green MG, her favorite travel mode, although she'd have to share the passenger seat with Rose, which wasn't a problem.

I slowed down a bit when we got close to Maggie's cottage. Her SUV was there, so I pulled in.

"Just a quick stop. Maggie left in a hurry this morning, so I want to find out if there was a problem," I explained.

"Left? What are you talking about?"

I filled Rose in about what had happened the night before, after she'd returned to her apartment.

"I was wondering why Bones was with you. He never leaves Maggie's side," Rose said.

"I'll just be a sec if you want to wait here with Pip," I said.

I knocked on the front door. No answer. I turned the doorknob, surprised that it wasn't locked. "Maggie?" I called after opening it.

She waved to me with one hand and held her phone to her ear with the other.

I walked through the entryway and stopped, shocked at the mess I saw. "What happened here?"

Maggie said goodbye and slid her phone into her back pocket. "Where's Bones?"

"At Sea Breeze with Luke, why? What's going on, Mags?"

"Someone broke in here last night, and as you can see, they trashed the place."

"The lottery ticket?" I asked, panicked that AJ left it here when they came to my house last night. I'd never even asked.

"AJ has it. He's sure that's what they were looking for. That and maybe Watson. I don't know, Dani. AJ came here this morning to check everything and found this mess." She waved her arm around the room. "Remember that we saw a car by your house last night? Well, AJ thinks maybe that same person broke in here when we left and returned to your house. At least that's his working theory for now."

"Is anything missing?"

Maggie grinned. "Interestingly, AJ had a plan in case anyone broke in. He left an envelope with the wrong lottery ticket inside as a decoy. Smart, huh? That's gone, so the joke's on whoever stole a dud. But it won't take long for them to figure out it's worthless."

"Do you have to stay here?"

"No. Where are you off to?"

"I'm going to the diner with Rose. She's pitching in today, so I can do some more nosing around. Want to come with me?" I knew what her answer would be.

She grabbed her jacket. "Are you kidding me? A tank of sharks couldn't keep me away. This stunt here makes me madder than a rooster in a blizzard and only makes me more determined to get to the bottom of what's going on."

"Meet me at the diner," I said and left.

Someone wanted that lottery ticket. What would they do next?

Chapter Twenty-Four

I ZIPPED INTO my small parking space between the Little Dog Diner and the Blueberry Bay Grapevine, happy no one had beaten me to it.

Maggie saw AJ loitering near the door to the Grapevine and headed in that direction.

Pip, Rose, and I entered the back door to my office. I gave her the small bowl of chicken with rice that Luke had prepared and told her I'd be right back. She knew the routine, had a comfy cushion, and I could count on her to stay out of the diner's kitchen and eating area.

Next, I checked in with Chad, my capable cook. He was busy plating pancakes with a side of fruit. Christie, Chad's wife and my reliable waitress, balanced several plates on her way out to the dining area to serve our hungry customers. I couldn't manage the diner without them.

"Rose is here to help out front," I said in passing.

"Already there," Chad said with a relieved smile. "She didn't waste any time grabbing an apron and getting to work. I never expected it to be so busy this morning." Chad slid three huge blueberry pancakes on a plate. "I think it has something to do with the murder yesterday. Everyone is buzzing with theories, and since it happened right next door, they think they'll have a front-row seat if anything else big happens."

"What," I said, chuckling with gallows humor. "Like another murder? What's wrong with people?"

Chad shrugged. "No idea. By the way, there's a customer who's been asking for you—dark hair, swept off his face, two-day stubble, wearing a hoodie. He finished eating, but he won't leave. He said he's not budging until you talk to him. Dani, we need the booth."

"Great," I mumbled. "Just what I don't need. You said he's done eating? I'll talk to him outside. At least that will get him out of your hair."

I bagged a couple of scones to use as a bribe and walked over to Gary's booth. "You're waiting to talk to me?"

He smiled, one of those evil grins that sent chills up my spine. "I thought you were avoiding me, Danielle Mackenzie."

"Not at all. I even brought you something to nibble on since you had to wait." I held up the bag. "I'm on my way out. I'll meet you out front."

He didn't budge. "Is that a polite brush-off? I don't plan to just go away."

"Not at all. I'll meet you outside," I repeated. "That is if you're serious about wanting to talk to me." I tilted my head and raised my brows, challenging him to meet my demand or get nothing. "I have to pick up my dog from my office."

He grabbed the bag out of my hand. "Fine."

I gave Pip the signal to follow me, and we walked around to the front of the diner. I found Gary leaning against the streetlight, and with his dark hoodie, he gave the impression of someone scoping out the area in preparation for committing a crime. Apparently, Pip agreed with me because I heard a low growl rumble from her chest. Something she saved for unsavory characters.

"So, Ms. Danielle Mackenzie," Gary said in a lazy drawl. "I have a proposition for you." My ears pricked up on high alert. "You have something I want, and I have information for you."

"I don't deal with thugs." I didn't try to hide my dislike of his presence.

Gary smirked. He nonchalantly ate some sunflower seeds and dropped the shells on the ground before saying, "Is that so? Is that how you compliment someone? No matter, I'll get right to the point. What do you know about the woman your grandmother sold the *Blueberry Bay Grapevine* to? Camilla Carter."

What was he talking about?

His gaze didn't leave my face. I forced myself to hide

my emotions, but apparently, not well enough.

"I see I've piqued your curiosity. Now, are you ready to talk?"

I crossed my arms. "What do you want, Gary? I'm not interested in playing games with you. If this is about your dog, the police are supervising his abandonment."

Gary laughed. "I don't care about the dog. Never did. That was all Thorne's thing. He loved his mutt more than anything, including his girlfriend. What a fool. No, I think you know what I want." He stared at me with his beady eyes until I had to look away.

"Dani? Is everything okay out here?" I breathed a sigh of relief at the sound of Maggie's tough, I-mean-business voice.

With Pip at my side and Maggie at my back, I squared my shoulders and said with confidence, "Everything's fine. Gary is just leaving."

He pushed away from the streetlight. "Okay, we'll play it your way, but I'll be back. Soon. You can count on it." He casually slicked his hair back and turned away from me.

I took several steps toward him, so he'd hear me loud and clear. "You couldn't control your half-brother, could you? Had to kill him to get your hands on his money, didn't you, Gary? But he suspected he was in danger and was a step ahead of you. I control that lottery ticket, and there's nothing you can do about it," I said, taunting him.

His shoulders stiffened, and he slowly turned around. The smirk was gone, replaced by a clamped jaw and squinty eyes.

He looked past me. "Before you go throwing around accusations, ask *her* if she had a reason to shut up my half-brother. And for the record, I want cold hard cash to keep quiet."

He walked to a small sedan and drove off.

I turned around. Cam, face white as a sheet, stood about five feet away, staring at me.

"Cam?" Maggie said, gently putting her arm around the older woman.

Cam's head dropped. "I thought I could leave all that behind me when I left Connecticut. Unfortunately, the past doesn't wash away just because I moved to the rocky coast of Maine."

I looped my arm through hers and led her toward her apartment. "Let's go inside and talk."

She let me lead her to her front door, unlocked it, and we followed her inside. She sank into a soft chair, leaving us to sit wherever. Pip pawed at Cam, and she patted her lap. Pip obliged. If anyone could lighten the mood, it was Pip, with her love for life and generous licks on the chin.

But despite Pip's attention, something was definitely off with Cam. "Is there anything you want to share?" I asked.

"Not really, but I suppose it's time I do." She sounded like her world had just shattered into a million pieces.

We gathered around Cam, waiting for her to work up her courage to open up.

"The thing is, I quit my old job because of an article I wrote about a stolen painting. I suspected insurance fraud that would put the owner of the painting in jail, but the more I dug into the details, the more someone stalked me. It was relentless. I was afraid he'd do anything to shut me up. But the worst part was the fear I felt at every corner, in every shadow, and around everyone walking near me. So, naively, I started using my maiden name and eventually left the city just to get my life back. Only it didn't work out like I'd hoped."

"Was that person Thorne Waite?" Maggie asked.

"No, but somehow, he dug up all the details. When Thorne and Gary showed up at the Grapevine's office, they told me I had to sell the business to them or they'd reveal everything, potentially bringing the stalker back into my life. It sounded farfetched so I called their bluff instead of going to the police for protection."

She scratched Pip under the chin, just where she loved it the most. "I thought I was smart enough to handle it on my own." She laughed. "Stupid of me."

Understandable, though. We always saw in hindsight where we could have acted differently. The important thing was to figure out where to go now.

"Cam, did you know it was Thorne lurking outside when you called yesterday morning?" I asked.

She shook her head in an attitude of regret. "I suspected, but even then, I really didn't expect him to take any action. I thought he was just trying to scare me, and it worked. And now Gary is still holding that information over my head. If Detective Crenshaw gets a whiff of Thorne's bullying, it gives him more reason to suspect me of murder." She sat so still I thought she was done talking, but then she blurted out, "What should I do?"

Maggie tapped her fingers on the arm of the chair, a sure sign she was processing this information. "To be clear, did you do something terrible to cause this, Cam?"

"No! It was my job."

"And you thought you'd left everything behind until Thorne and Gary approached you," I said.

"Exactly. They said they wanted the *Grapevine* in exchange for their silence. Of course, they offered a pittance to make it look legit. Now, Gary just told you he wants cash."

"Blackmail. I only see one thing for you to do, Cam. Talk to Detective Crenshaw. Tell him what happened," Maggie said, not understanding the situation from Cam's perspective.

"Are you kidding me? He'll throw me in jail, and the real killer will walk away free as a bird."

"She has a point, Mags. AJ still has the lottery ticket, right? Let's use it to our advantage, flush out that no-good killer." I said with no compassion.

Cam stood up and paced across her living room like a cornered rat. "I don't want you to put yourselves in danger for me. That's not acceptable. There has to be another way."

"Here's how I see it, Cam," I said. "Thorne and Gary approached Luna's Labradors and bought two puppies. One has a genetic disorder. Luna told me that Thorne was going to get you to write a negative article about her business to ruin her. Supposedly, they wanted her business, also. Now you tell us they planned to reveal your identity unless you sold them the *Blueberry Bay Grapevine*. So, what were they up to?"

"Fishing for any scheme that worked to get something for nothing?" Cam said. "I don't know anything about Luna's Labradors, and I wouldn't print an article without a lot of research."

"That's it! Fishing for a scheme and pitting Luna against you, Cam. But I think it was mostly Gary scheming. Think about it. Thorne left you that note apologizing for his dog pooping on your walk. I think Thorne had a change of heart about being involved in his half-brother's criminal schemes, and he wanted to warn you about Gary's underhanded information about Luna," I said, seeing the pieces starting to make sense.

"Great point," Maggie said. "Thorne didn't need money. Gary probably pressured him to set him up with something, but Thorne got cold feet. Dani, he told you the lottery ticket ruined his life, and he thought he was in danger. That's why he left the ticket with you. Thorne wasn't the problem, but he paid with his life."

Cam looked between Maggie and me. "So, you think Gary killed his own half-brother?"

"Maybe. He definitely wanted money. But so did Thorne's ex-girlfriend, Lyndsey. She didn't conduct herself very well last night at my house. You heard her, Cam. Without much prying, she revealed her true colors."

"She pretended to come along to do an interview. At least I'm done with her now." Cam said, sounding relieved.

"And Luna had a motive to save her business. She didn't know Thorne was going to warn you. She thought he was going to tell you something to destroy what she'd worked so hard to build."

I stood up and looked out the window at Main Street. Was someone out there now plotting more misdeeds?

Pip scratched at the door, telling me she needed to go out.

"Cam, stay here and lock your doors. Someone stole a phony lottery ticket last night. The culprit will be furious when they discover it's a dud if they haven't already. I know it will be hard but try not to worry. We'll get to the bottom of this."

I usually didn't give someone false hope, but in this case, I had to give Cam something to hang onto.

Even if I wasn't sure I could pull it off.

Chapter Twenty-Five

MAGGIE, PIP, AND I left Cam barricaded in her apartment. I hoped I hadn't scared her half to death with my warning. She'd had enough concerns in her previous life. As long as she stayed put, or at least didn't venture out alone, I didn't think she had to worry about Gary running around like a loose cannon.

"What's your plan, Dani?" Maggie said while we waited for Pip to find the right spot to do her business behind the diner. The Pipster was fussy about that detail. First, she had to sniff everything, and then she'd disappear behind a bush to finish. Nothing wrong with needing privacy, but sometimes, like right now, I wished she'd just hurry it up.

I glanced up at Cam's apartment window. The blind was closed. Good. She'd taken our warning to heart.

"Mags?" I asked to distract myself from waiting on Pip. "Did AJ find anything to help figure out who broke into your cottage last night?"

She snorted. "Yeah, a pile of sunflower seed shells on

the table. He said he'd get me some mouse traps to deal with that problem. Isn't that one reason to have a cat? Radar's slacking on her job, I guess." She shrugged as if to imply what could she do?

My heart sped up. "Mags? Maybe you don't have a mouse. Gary was eating sunflower seeds when I talked to him earlier. I bet he broke into your cottage and dropped shells there, too."

"What a slob!"

Pip finally peed but then started digging like we had nothing better to do but watch as she sent dirt flying every which way.

"Pip!" I said. "Come on!"

I could have been talking to myself for all the attention she paid me.

Frustrated, I moved closer, digging in my pocket for a treat to distract her from her excavation. Instead of a treat though, I felt the silver pendant I'd found the day before. I'd forgotten all about it.

Just then, Maggie bent down and searched in the grass. "Hey, Dani, take a look at this." She held up a beaded necklace for my inspection. "Doesn't Lyndsey wear lots of jewelry like this? I found it right near where Pip was digging."

I draped the blue and green beads over my fingers. "She does. And I found this yesterday." I showed Maggie the pendant. "How did it get here?"

"Or, when?" Maggie said with a glint in her eyes and a glance toward the *Grapevine's* office. "Are you thinking what I'm thinking?"

"Absolutely. We need to find Lyndsey. But where might she be?"

I shoved the necklace and pendant in my pocket. We needed to get moving. Pip looked at me with her big brown eyes as if to say *what's the big deal?* I scooped her into my arms, dirty feet, and all, and kissed her head, then put her back down. I could never stay upset with my quirky Pipster, and she knew it.

Distracted from her digging, Pip trotted toward Main Street. She clearly had a destination in mind, and we had to jog to keep up. She stopped at the light pole in front of the Little Dog Diner where Gary had been and sniffed around.

I dragged the toe of my sneaker through the bark mulch, uncovering a pile of sunflower seed shells. "See?" I said to Maggie. "Gary's mess."

It wasn't long before Pip lost interest in that spot and trotted off down the sidewalk.

"Where is she going now?"

"I don't know, Mags, but her nose is to the ground. She's picked up a scent. First, the necklace, then the sunflower seed shells. She's leading us somewhere."

We followed Pip, butt swaying back and forth as she trotted straight past the Little Dog Diner and the Cut n'

Curl. Eventually, she stopped in front of the door to the Hidden Treasures souvenir shop and scratched.

"Is she telling you she needs a new bandana or something?" Maggie joked.

I hoped it was more important than that.

Suddenly, the door flew open. Lyndsey charged out, yelling over her shoulder, "Don't bother calling, I don't want to work here anyway."

I snatched Pip out of the way just before Lyndsey tripped over her. Clearly, she wasn't looking where she was going.

"Lyndsey? Everything okay?"

"Of course not," she snapped. "Cam fired me. No one will hire me, and it's all your fault, so just get out of my way." She shoved past me as she tied a sweatshirt around her waist.

How was any of this my fault?

Maggie stepped in front of her and shoved her hand in the middle of Lyndsey's chest. "Slow down. You lost that job all by yourself, so I suggest you apologize before I—"

"You what?" Lyndsey shouted, braids flaring out as she twisted in Maggie's direction.

Clearly, emotions were running high. That wouldn't help anyone. Especially since I wanted information.

I pulled Maggie's arm back and addressed Lyndsey as calmly as I could. "Last night, when you and Cam came to my house, it was confusing. We worried about what would happen to the two black Labs, and I took my frustration out on you. Maybe it should have been directed toward Gary."

Maggie glared at me, clearly disagreeing, but I shook my head, and she backed off.

I pointed across the street. "How about we sit down on that bench, enjoy the view, and talk everything over. What do you think?" I held my breath because I didn't have a backup plan if she refused.

"Will *you* give me a job?" she asked, sounding desperate.

I thought about Rose filling in and knew that wasn't ideal. "On a trial basis," I said.

Maggie looked at me as if I'd lost my mind, but if offering a job was the only way to get Lyndsey to talk to us, so be it.

We crossed the street and sat on the well-worn wooden bench. This spot, a favorite of the locals, provided a path between the buildings and the rocky shore. Pip scrambled over the rocks and ran to the water as if she were visiting a long-lost friend.

I put my hand in my pocket and rubbed the pendant. "You've had a rough couple of days, haven't you, Lyndsey?"

She rolled her eyes. "Boy, that's an understatement. One thing after the other, right? I'm ready to jump off this roller coaster and just leave town. But I can't yet. I can't abandon Thorne until after the funeral. I mean, we broke up and all, and he's dead, but still, I want closure. You know what I mean?"

I definitely knew what she meant. I was after closure, too, but from a different angle. And I was happy she was ready to babble.

"What happened between you and Thorne?" Maggie asked, now on board with my approach.

Lyndsey flipped her wrist dismissively. "That dog. Thorne loved that dog more than he cared about me. You know?" She twisted around to look at me. "It was humiliating, but I've moved on."

I pulled out the necklace and pendant. "I found this and wondered if they're yours. You wear a lot of jewelry like this."

She took them out of my hand to study them. "I haven't seen them for a month, at least. Thorne bought them for me at Creative Design, but when we broke up, I left some of my stuff in his apartment. I didn't want the memory. Where did you find this?" She handed the handful of pieces back to me. "Keep it."

"Near the Little Dog Diner," I said. "Pip led us to it. She was digging in the flower bed near the side door."

"That's weird." Then Lyndsey's eyes widened. "But you know who was in and out of Thorne's apartment all the time? Gary. I bet he dropped them."

"Why would he have your things?" Maggie asked.

"He was always stealing stuff from Thorne. Who knows why? He'd stick stuff in his pocket just because. I think it's a sickness."

That fit in with our theory that he broke into Maggie's apartment. We sat in silence, except for the few cars driving by and the sound of the crashing waves.

"So, when can I start working at the diner? I don't wash pots. Wrecks my nails. And no clearing tables unless you don't care if I drop stuff. I'm a clumsy mess."

"Gee, that only leaves picking out lobster meat for the lobster rolls, right Dani?" Maggie said without a trace of sarcasm.

"Yup. I could use you tomorrow for a few hours."

Lyndsey stood up, turned, and faced me. "You're joking, right?"

A wet Pip ran to the bench and shook, drenching Lyndsey's pants. She jumped away and shrieked. "What's wrong with your dog?"

Maggie faked a cough to hide her laugh.

"Sorry. Pip doesn't usually let herself get soaked by the waves. I guess her timing was off today. And, no, I'm not joking about cracking the lobster shells. If that doesn't work for you, no problem," I said, silently thanking Maggie for suggesting the task in the first place. It got me out of a jam.

Lyndsey wiped at the splatter on her yoga pants but

only made it worse when the sand and water smeared into a gray mess. "Cracking lobsters sounds disgusting. Remind me never to eat at your diner again," she said and stalked off.

Thank goodness I wouldn't have to worry about shells in my lobster rolls.

"Wait," Maggie called and jogged after her. "So, I think Gary broke into my cottage last night. Do you know where we can find him?"

"He what? Why?"

Maggie laughed since the reason was obvious to us. "Looking to steal something? I don't know, but he took a worthless lottery ticket. The winning one is secure with Dani. Anyway, we want to ask him a few questions about this misadventure in my cottage."

Lyndsey snorted and shook her head. "Worthless, huh? That kind of thing always happens in Gary's world. Try Thorne's apartment. Gary moaned and complained about how expensive the Blue Moon Inn was. He called it highway robbery. To be honest? I wouldn't be surprised if he skipped out without paying."

Even more reason to find him, I thought.

Chapter Twenty-Six

I WATCHED LYNDSEY saunter off as if she hadn't a care in the world. As far as I could tell, her job prospects were dim, considering her attitude and aversion to doing actual work. Oh well. Not my problem.

Maggie returned to the bench and sat with a weary sigh. "What do you make of Pip bringing us on this jaunt after finding Lyndsey's bracelet?"

At the sound of her name, Pip cocked her head.

"I wish she could tell us, but we'll have to be smart and figure it out ourselves, Mags. If what Lyndsey said about Gary stealing her bracelet from Thorne's apartment is true, did he drop it intentionally or by accident?"

"Yeah, I was wondering the same thing. The bracelet makes for a good red herring if Gary wants to draw attention away from himself, right? Maybe he followed Thorne yesterday morning, ready to confront him about the lottery ticket, and everything went sideways."

I drew my brows together, deep in thought for a moment. "Gary said he was meeting Thorne to walk

Bones. I think he just let Bones go and followed Thorne into the *Grapevine's* office. We know what happened there."

Maggie nodded. "What should we do next?"

I snapped my fingers to get Pip's attention. "At some point, we should drive by Thorne's apartment and see if there's any activity. Just to keep tabs on Gary."

"If he hasn't flown the coop like Lyndsey suggested."

"I doubt he's gone. Gary wants that lottery ticket. We'll have to be clever since he was already tricked twice, assuming he's the one who broke into your cottage, Mags," I said.

"The dogs wouldn't have escaped if it was Luna, so we can cross her off the list. I'd like to have another chat with her and clear the air around Bones and Watson, though. I don't want to worry that she'll pull out that contract and undermine me again."

"Good point. Once I offer to use the lottery money to help finance her dog training, I think she'll be in our back pocket forever. Let's go."

Pip heard me say *let's go*, and she was already waiting at the crosswalk. She understood me even if I didn't always understand her. I definitely had room for improvement in that area.

Before we made it back to my car, Trudy Moore shouted, "Dani? Dani Mackenzie? Did Detective Crenshaw find that beautiful dog?"

We both turned around to face a middle-aged woman wearing large glasses trying to catch up to us.

"Who's she?" Maggie whispered.

The friendly woman stopped next to me. While she caught her breath, I said, "Hi, Trudy. This is my friend Maggie. Maggie, this is Trudy Moore, friends with Lyndsey," I added.

"Well, I wouldn't go as far as to say we're friends. It turns out Lyndsey's not really my type."

"Oh? I've seen you together at the diner," I said, hoping she'd elaborate.

Trudy snorted. "We met there a couple of times, but she always ran off and left me with the bill. I won't make *that* mistake again."

Maggie quickly glanced at me. I looped my arm through Trudy's. "We're heading to the Little Dog Diner. How does coffee and a blueberry muffin sound?"

"Scrumptious. And is this your cute pup? I've seen her outside the diner, sitting in the sun with her adorable bandana on. What's your name, honey?"

"That's Pip. Do you have a dog, Trudy?" I asked as we walked together.

"Not at the moment. My Miss Mocha crossed the rainbow bridge a month ago. That's why I was so upset when I heard about the dog that got lost from the Blue Moon Inn. Did anyone find him?"

I patted her hand resting on my forearm. "Yes. He's

just fine, and I'll be happy to tell you that the irresponsible person who abandoned Watson will never get him back."

Her eyes lit up. "Is he looking for a home?"

"That's up in the air for now, but I'll let Detective Crenshaw know you're interested," Maggie said.

Trudy gave Maggie a hip check. "Ooh-la-la! I saw you with that handsome detective at the inn. Such a cute couple! He proposed last night, didn't he?"

Maggie smiled, then held out her hand to let her engagement ring sparkle in the sunshine. "He did and I couldn't be happier."

"I always say that when you find a good man, hang on to him through blizzards and hurricanes. Now, for that coffee?"

I liked Trudy. She knew what she wanted, and she called a spade a spade. When we reached the diner, I held the door open for her. Rose saw us and gestured toward an empty booth.

"Go ahead and sit down over there. My grandmother will bring you coffee. I have to take Pip to my office." I curved my hand around my mouth. "Some people don't like to see her in here while they're eating."

"Ridiculous," Trudy said. "Anyone can see that your little Pip is well-behaved and wouldn't bother anyone. Right, Pip?" she said in a high voice.

Pip wagged her stubby tail, thrilled with all the attention, but I scooped her into my arms and walked to my office. Once Pip was settled in her bed with a treat, I popped my head into the kitchen.

"Everything good here, Chad?"

He gave me two thumbs up. "Smooth as the bay on a calm day, Dani."

That was what I wanted to hear. I put an assortment of muffins on a plate and joined Maggie and Trudy, just as she said, "Poor Thorne was heartbroken when Lyndsey told him she was done with him."

I pushed the plate in front of Trudy. She wasn't shy about helping herself.

"She told me that he cared more about that dog than her. You know what? I don't blame him. That dog of his was the sweetest boy. And Lyndsey? Well, never mind, I don't like to speak badly about anyone."

Maggie beamed. "Bones is definitely a sweetie, but so much more, Trudy. I plan to give him the best home he could ever wish for."

"Thorne would be happy. You know, he seemed kind of distracted the last time I talked to him."

"You were friends?"

"Neighbors, actually. We shared a duplex, and I couldn't have asked for a more helpful neighbor. He took my garbage out, helped me with my groceries, and even offered to water my plants if I went away. Lyndsey sure let a good one go. And, for what? Money. She wanted a chunk of money from that ticket he won, and when he told her he was going to use it to help dogs, she about blew her top. Same with his half-brother. If you ask me, Thorne got all the kindness genes in that family."

Trudy finished her muffin and reached for another. "Aren't you girls having one?"

"Maybe later," Maggie said.

"Actually, we need to go, but you should stay as long as you like. Ask Rose for a refill if you need more coffee," I said. "And don't be shy about dropping in again, Trudy. Pip would love to see you."

Trudy grabbed my hand. "I will, and thank you, dear. You made my day. I was beginning to think I'd lost the one person in town I could count on." She wiped a tear away.

After Maggie and I slid out of the booth, I thought of another question. "Trudy, did you notice if anyone was in Thorne's apartment last night?"

She thought for a minute. "I heard something, kind of muffled, but didn't give it too much thought. It could have come from outside. I suppose. I hope that handsome detective finds the murderer soon. It's kind of creepy to think a killer is on the loose."

"Just remember to lock your doors. I'll ask Detective Crenshaw to do a drive-by on your street if that will make you feel better," Maggie said.

"Would you? You're a dear."

Trudy's phone rang, giving us the perfect opportunity to exit without feeling guilty.

I woke Pip up from her nap and brought her outside to Maggie. "You know what I think we should do, Mags?"

"Yeah. Do a stake out from Trudy's apartment. Kind of a no-brainer, Dani."

"Great minds think alike."

We both laughed.

"First, though, I need to talk to Luna and let her know about the plan for the lottery ticket money. Are you coming?"

Maggie hemmed and hawed. "I'd like to see Bones, but I don't want you going by yourself so, okay. I'll follow you, but I'm heading straight to Sea Breeze afterwards."

"Deal," I said and slipped behind the wheel of the MG.

"Ready, Pip?" She looked at me as if I'd just asked the dumbest question ever. She yipped, telling me to get moving already.

I backed out, with Maggie following behind.

How would this meeting with Luna go?

Chapter Twenty-Seven

Luna's Labradors was as still as a pile of sleeping puppies when we arrived. I parked next to Luna's van, and Maggie stated the obvious as we looked for another human being. "No dogs are barking or anything."

We stood next to each other facing the kennel, and I could only echo her sentiments. "Yeah, kind of eerie. What do you think is going on?"

We didn't have to wait long before the kennel door opened. Luna walked out carrying a bucket, dirt smudged on her face, and jeans torn at her knees. She stopped, a scowl darkening her face.

"What are you two doing here? Haven't you done enough harm already?" She put the bucket down and crossed her arms. "I know how you got your boyfriend to intervene on your behalf to keep Sherlock and Watson. Detective Winter was ready to send them back here where they belong."

I took a step toward Luna.

"Stop right there! I don't want you on this property." She pulled out her phone.

I held up my hand. "Wait, Luna. I think you'll want to hear what I have to say."

"I doubt it, but I'll give you five minutes. I could use a good laugh on this chaotic day," she said, her phone still held at the ready.

Pip finished investigating the interesting smells near the cars and made a beeline straight over to Luna. I held my breath. Would she lash out at my pipsqueak or welcome her?

Luna startled, then she crouched down and gave Pip a hearty back scratch. "You're a cutie pie," she said, not holding any grudge against Pip, even though she wanted us out of her sight.

I exhaled and sent Pip a silent thank-you for helping us navigate this difficult situation.

"Luna? I have a proposal to make."

She dug in her pocket and held out a small treat for Pip. "Yeah, spit it out."

"Maggie and I are impressed with your Labradors, your business, your hard work. It can't be easy, and we'd like to help."

"Help? Yeah right. You're probably just like the Waite brothers and want to steal it all. No thanks!"

I shook my head and stepped closer. "No. Nothing like that. Honestly, we want to help financially. Thorne left me his winning lottery ticket in case something happened to him. He knew his life was in danger, but he still made a plan for the money. He wanted it used to help dogs."

"That's right," Maggie said, jumping into the conversation before Luna could shoo us off her property. "And because of Sherlock Bones's condition, and the fact that he's such an incredible and compassionate dog, we thought a partnership to train dogs any way you think best would be the perfect complement to your business. You told us that some of your dogs don't meet the high standards for the seeing-eye program. With this money, more of your pups could be trained to help people with other needs."

Luna's eyes teared up. "You aren't here to take everything away from me?"

"Absolutely not. But Maggie hopes to keep Sherlock Bones."

"With your help training him, of course," Maggie quickly added. "I want to learn from you if you need a helper."

Luna stood stock-still, too emotional to speak.

Pip, however, ran around in circles, yipping and yapping as if she knew something special had just happened. And of course, her barking got all the Labradors in the kennel adding their voices to hers, creating quite a loud, but happy, dog chorus that chased away all eeriness from our arrival.

"What about Thorne?" Luna asked. "Has the killer been found, or am I still a suspect?"

I shouldn't have been surprised that she was still on edge. Who wouldn't be?

"Not yet. *We* don't think you killed him, Luna. Especially, after talking to Cam. If Thorne had given her negative information about your business, she would have followed up with in-depth-research before she published anything. You followed the protocols for the seizure disorder, so you don't have a motive to cover up anything. It was all lies and bullying on Gary and Thorne's part."

Luna's body relaxed. Her shoulders sagged, and she let out a loud sigh. "Thank you. Come on while I finish up inside."

Maggie grinned at me after Luna turned around and opened the kennel door, holding it open for us. Pip charged inside first and ran straight to the puppy pen, stubby tail wagging so fast her whole butt wiggled with happiness. It was obvious she wanted to check them out. Who wouldn't?

"Why not?" Luna said and unhooked the latch. "These puppies haven't seen any other dogs yet, and Pip is the perfect first friend for them."

While Pip let the six pups sniff and jump on her, Luna got back to her cleaning chores in the puppy pen.

"I already cleaned the other kennels while the dogs were in their outside run, but they know something is going on in here." She hit a button that raised five doors at the back of each kennel. Five black Labradors bounded inside, barking, wagging tails, and slobbering.

"Maggie, taking care of these dogs is a lot of work. Are you up to it?" Luna stroked Sasha, obviously, her favorite, as she waited for a reply.

My friend who had more energy than a greyhound, laughed. "Work? That's my middle name. Seriously, you won't find a harder worker. Plus, I'm head over heels in love with Bones. I don't know what it is about that dog, but the minute he sat on my lap when we picked him up from the middle of the road, I knew we were destined to be together. Does that sound weird?"

"Not at all. Happens all the time." Luna raised her eyebrows. "Where is he now?"

"He's at Dani's house, and honestly, I feel naked without him. Someone tried to steal Bones and Watson last night, so now we make sure they're always supervised." Maggie held a puppy between her neck and shoulder, letting the pup lick her cheek.

"Who would do that?" Luna asked, horror at the idea draining the color from her cheeks.

I stammered before I admitted, "We thought it might have been you. Gary left Watson in his room unsupervised, and he escaped. Someone at the inn said they saw a van like yours on the street."

Indignation brought the color back to Luna's face. "It wasn't me," she said fiercely. "I don't have the time or energy to wait around in case a dog escapes. Besides, I didn't even know Watson was at the Blue Moon Inn."

I picked up a puppy that had been trying to climb my leg.

I smiled, wanting to reassure Luna that we believed her. "We know. We think Gary broke into Maggie's cottage, maybe to steal the dogs, or else he was looking for something else. We aren't sure. Fortunately, both dogs escaped and ran straight to my house. As you know, it's a short run if you're on the beach. Bones knew the way."

Luna shuddered. "Stealing dogs? That's awful."

"Yeah, and there was a second break-in," Maggie said. "Last night, we found someone lurking around Dani's house, so AJ and I took the dogs and stayed with her. This morning, I found my cottage totally trashed."

Luna leaned against Sasha's gate. "You're kidding? This is going too far. And for what?"

"We're sure it's about the winning lottery ticket," I said. "Maybe you can help us."

Luna shook her head in disbelief. "I don't know. I already ended up in the middle of a mess I want nothing to do with. I just like to hang out with my dogs; mind my own business."

"Okay. I get it," I said, giving her time to think about the situation.

Sometimes, that was all someone needed to come around.

Luna looked up and gave me a soulful look. "I should at least hear you out. What do you have in mind?" she asked tentatively.

I looked at Maggie. We hadn't really discussed a plan, so I quickly formed one on the spot.

"Everything keeps looping back to Gary. How about you contact him tomorrow. Tell him you're ready to kill the story he threatened to bring to Cam to publish."

"It's a nothing story, though," she said.

"Of course it is, but he doesn't know what we know. The goal is to trap him. You tell him that I've offered you a lot of money to buy your business, and you can't risk any bad publicity ahead of the sale. Tell him I'll have the money after I cash in the lottery ticket. Tell him you'll pay him in twenty-four hours to shut down the story about Sherlock's seizures. Tell him I bragged to you about having Thorne's winning lottery ticket, and I'd do whatever I wanted with the money. And that means buying your business. Add that you're out of money, and you have no option but to sell."

"But I don't have any money to pay him. This won't work."

"You don't actually give him money or even meet

with him. The point is that we want to catch him in the act of stealing the lottery ticket."

"I don't know," Luna said. "This sounds too dangerous. If he already killed his half-brother, how will you be safe?"

"Let us worry about that part, Luna," Maggie said. "All you have to do is make a phone call."

"But what if he comes here? What do I do then?"

She had a good point. One I hadn't thought about, but Maggie quickly came up with a plan.

"Call Detective Winter tomorrow and tell her someone has been threatening you. Ask her to drive by and look around," Maggie suggested.

We all nodded our heads at the brilliance of Maggie's plan.

I added, "And I'll ask my friend Sue Ellen to stay with you starting tonight just so you have some company. Believe me, she'll put the fear of the almighty into anyone who shows up. They'll wish they'd never crossed her path."

"Okay. I'll keep Sasha and the puppies inside with me and lock up the kennel. It has an alarm system that's routed straight to the police station," she said, talking through her new strategy.

"Great!" Maggie said and hugged Luna. "We'll get this sorted out and then get to the job of training your puppies. I can't wait!"

I looked at the chaos of puppies around Pip. "Do you want help bringing them into your house?" I asked.

"That would be great. Everything is all set here. The kennels are clean, and the dogs have food and water."

We each cradled two puppies in our arms. Luna set the alarm, and with Sasha and Pip following, we trailed Luna into her house. Releasing the puppies into her spacious country kitchen gave them a new burst of energy. They chased Pip, then each other, then their tails. It was nonstop puppy pandemonium but in a very entertaining way. To be honest? I didn't want to leave.

"I'd offer you something to eat, but I haven't had any time to think about food," Luna said, sounding slightly embarrassed. "Lately, I've been living on bagels with cream cheese and fruit."

"Don't worry. I'll text Sue Ellen right now and tell her to bring food."

An embarrassed flush crossed her face. "This all sounds like so much trouble."

"No trouble at all. I want you to be comfortable and not worry about anything until this mess is over. Understand?" I gave her my most serious expression.

My phone beeped with an incoming message. "Sue Ellen is on her way," I said. "With food. I don't know what she's bringing, but I'm guessing it will be some kind of gourmet feast."

Luna sagged with relief. "I don't know how I'll ever

thank you. One minute, I'm looking over my shoulder, wondering when I'll be arrested for a murder I didn't commit, and the next, I'm treated like royalty with food and money. Am I dreaming?"

Maggie laughed. "Nope."

Now all we had to do was hope my impromptu plan worked to scoop up a killer.

Chapter Twenty-Eight

MAGGIE, DESPERATE TO reunite with Bones, headed back to fetch him at Sea Breeze. I needed to check in at the diner and get ready for tomorrow morning. Juggling my responsibilities at the diner plus unraveling threads surrounding Thorne's murder was a lot. Hopefully, it ended soon.

Pip curled up on the passenger seat, instead of riding with her paws on the dash like usual.

"Your new friends ran you ragged today, didn't they, Pip?"

She opened one eye, but that was all she could manage. I knew how she felt because I was running on empty myself.

I pulled into my spot next to the diner, hoping I'd find everything in order.

But first, before going inside, I called Luke.

"Hey. I'm at the diner, then I'll be home. Should I bring dinner?"

"Nope. There are enough leftovers from Lily's extravaganza that we won't have to cook for a week."

"Perfect. See you in a bit," I said and hung up.

I left Pip curled up on the passenger seat, let myself into the diner, and flipped on the light. I took a moment to let the quiet wash over me before walking into the kitchen. Predictably, Chad had left it spotless. The booths and counter sparkled, thanks to Christy's efficient skills. I sighed. I couldn't be luckier with these two capable and reliable employees.

A loud rap on the diner door made me flinch. Had someone followed me here?

I peeked out the window. Cam stood on the stoop, awash in the overhead light, fidgeting and looking around like she expected someone to jump out from the shadows. Pip sat next to her, looking up at me.

I opened the door. "Come in, Cam. Is everything okay?"

"As good as can be expected, I guess," she said "I've been holed up in my apartment all day, and when I saw the light come on, I decided to brave the few steps to come over here. Pip must have heard me. She barked, so I let her out of your car. I hope that's okay?

"Of course." I scooped up the Pipster to let her know she hadn't been abandoned.

"Can I beg you for something to eat? Anything at all."

"Of course. Let's go in the kitchen and see what's

there." I felt guilty that I'd scared her earlier, and she'd been afraid to venture outside, but better safe than sorry.

"Lyndsey called me begging for another chance to work on an article. I have to say she sounded like she'd learned a lesson but also sounded desperate," Cam said almost as if she wanted my opinion but was afraid to come right out and ask what she should do.

I opened the walk-in cooler and found leftovers from my birthday breakfast wrapped up and labeled with Lily's flowery script. "How about some fruit pizza and a piece of quiche?"

"Perfect. Thank you. I was actually desperate to talk to someone even more than have a bite to eat, but now that I'm thinking about food, I'm starving.

We sat at a small table in the kitchen, instead of messing up the counter in the dining area.

I unwrapped the containers and pushed them toward Cam. "You know, you can do whatever you want about Lyndsey, but if you want my opinion, I think she only cares about herself. So, be very careful. She's also opinionated about which jobs she'll actually do. My guess? She'll want the best assignments."

"I had that same impression. I'm not going to promise anything until this whole Thorne mess is behind me anyway." Cam picked up a sliver of fruit pizza and took a bite. "Oh my, even left over, this is delicious."

"Speaking of Thorne, I talked to Luna earlier. I told

her I planned to use the lottery ticket money to help her with her dog training. Maggie is jumping in with both feet to help, too. That would make a good article and give Luna's Labradors a much-needed publicity boost. A business can't beat good press."

Cam nodded. "I can do that." She gave a piece of crust to Pip then wiped crumbs off her fingers before digging into the quiche. I got her a glass of water and put a bowl on the floor for Pip.

"Want to take anything back to your apartment?"

She waved off that suggestion. "Oh no. This was perfect. And thank you for giving me some of your time. I'm sure you want to get home yourself." She stood up and walked to the door. "Thanks again, Dani," she said and headed into the darkness.

"Just you and me, Pip. Before we leave, I want to look in the cooler and check what needs to be done first thing in the morning."

I looked at the items that Chad had carefully labeled and lined up on shelves, then checked the pastry display. Next, I opened the notebook on the corner desk and jotted a few notes for him when he arrived in the morning—*MORE BLUEBERRY MUFFINS, APPLE SCONES, AND LEMON TARTS FOR THE PASTRY DISPLAY, ANOTHER BATCH OF CLAM CHOWDER AND PLENTY OF CHOPPED VEGGIES FOR SALADS. THANK YOU!*

"That ought to do it, Pip. Ready to go home?"

She yipped and ran to the door.

I switched off the light, opened it, and came face-to-face with Gary.

I screamed, then slammed and locked the door. Shaking and with my heart racing, I sagged against the doorjamb. Pip jumped against the door, over and over, scratching and yipping.

I managed to fumble my phone out of my pocket and dial 911.

As soon as the dispatcher answered, I whispered, my voice shaky, "This is Dani Mackenzie. Someone is trying to break into the Little Dog Diner. I'm locked inside."

"I'll send someone right away. Are you okay?"

"Yes. Please hurry."

"Stay on the phone. Is the person still at the door?"

"I don't know."

I'm not sure I'd hear anything over the pounding of my heart. I clutched the phone to my ear and slid down until I was sitting on the floor. Pip wiggled into my arms, and I hugged her like she was my lifeline.

"It'll be okay, Pip," I said, more for my benefit than hers.

Finally, after what seemed like forever, but was probably only minutes, I heard a siren. I sucked in a deep breath, counted to ten, and slowly let it out. Lights flooded the inside of the diner.

"Dani Mackenzie? Are you inside?"

I slowly inched my way up and peeked out the window. Detective Jane Winter was on the other side, her hands cupped around her face, looking in. I flung the door open, never happier to see her. She stepped in next to me.

"Dani? Tell me what happened while Detective Crenshaw checks outside." She turned on the light and gently guided me to one of the counter stools. "Sit down. Take your time."

I took a deep breath and said, "I came to check that everything was all set for tomorrow. Cam walked over. I gave her some food, and we talked for a few minutes. Then, I wrote a note for Chad listing items for him to check on in the morning. Pip and I were ready to leave, but when I opened the door, I saw someone standing in the shadows. I think it was Gary Waite."

"You aren't sure?" she asked, but kindly, not in her usual brusque manner.

I shook my head. "The outside motion light wasn't on. He wore a dark sweatshirt with the hood up that made him hard to identify."

Jane scribbled as fast as I spoke. Just as we finished, AJ walked inside.

He took my hands in his. "Dani? Your hands are ice cold, and you're shaking like a leaf. Look at me. I didn't find anything outside except your light is broken. It must have happened recently because there's still glass near the door from the broken bulb. Did you notice that when you walked inside tonight?"

"No. The light was working when Cam came over. I'm positive."

"Okay. Let's lock up and I'll drive you home. Detective Winter? I'd like you to take one more look around. And check with Camilla, too. Maybe she noticed something from her apartment."

Jane nodded. "I'll see you tomorrow, Detective."

That was the best plan I'd heard all day.

Chapter Twenty-Nine

AJ DROVE MY MG. I held Pip tight to my chest, my body tense as I stared straight ahead.

"I panicked, AJ. It was such a shock to see that person standing at the door when I opened it. I totally panicked."

Now that it was behind me, the tears started.

AJ reached over and squeezed my shoulder. "A normal reaction, Dani. Especially after all that has happened. I'm just glad you're okay. Do you know what Maggie would do to me if something had happened to you?"

I snorted through my sobbing. "That would be nothing compared to what Rose and Luke would do."

AJ let out an exaggerated groan. "You're right. No one would ever find my body again."

"AJ? Thanks for making me laugh."

After that, we drove in silence for a few minutes before I said, "I think it was Gary, but I'm just not positive. Who else could it be?"

"Are you sure it wasn't Cam?"

"I'm sure. She came over before this happened. I gave her some food, and she left. It wasn't her."

"Lyndsey? She's a bit unpredictable."

"I don't think so."

"Maybe in the morning, after a good night's sleep, some new detail will click. Now, everything is a blur," he said, trying to reassure me.

"Sleep? I'll never be able to get to sleep."

AJ didn't say anything. I was glad he didn't argue or tell me everything would be fine, or worse, say it was all in my imagination. Even Jane had been kind and showed more compassion than I'd ever seen. Maybe she wasn't so bad after all.

"That stupid lottery ticket," I mumbled. "Thorne said it ruined his life. Maybe I'm cursed now."

AJ pulled into my driveway. The lights glowing through the windows cast a warm, welcoming aura that wrapped around me and somehow made me think I'd safely get through this.

"Dani? I called Luke and told him what happened, so you won't have to retell it all again. Maggie and Rose are here, so we'll all sit down, relax, and have a late dinner. Sound good?"

"It sounds normal, AJ. Normal is good."

Luke was the first one to hear the front door open, and he had me in his arms before both of my feet were inside. He lifted me off the floor and rocked me back and forth.

"I wanted to come to the diner when AJ called, but he said he was bringing you home and insisted I wait here. Are you alright?"

He set me down and searched my face. What did he see? Fear? I hoped not.

I melted into his strong arms. "I'm starving. You said something about leftovers?"

Luke chuckled. "You must by okay if you're thinking about food."

Rose pulled me away from Luke and gave me one of her hugs that felt like it would never end. She didn't have to say anything, I knew exactly what she was thinking. She'd move every grain of sand to keep me safe.

Maggie handed me a glass of wine, and I accepted it gratefully.

Of course, Bones and Watson added their welcome by jumping on me. I stumbled back and spilled half the wine, but who cared? I was home.

The rest of the evening passed in a blur of eating, drinking, and laughing. But all the while, I couldn't shake the image of the hooded person standing in the dark on the Little Dog Diner step.

Was it Gary?

Despite my concern, I slept well and got out of bed the next morning, feeling like I could tackle anything.

Luke hovered over me as if he was afraid I might fall apart at any minute.

As we sat together in the kitchen, me with lemon tea and Luke with black coffee, I told him the plan Maggie and I concocted with Luna the day before.

"Okay," he said. "But you aren't going to put yourself out there like a target all by yourself, Dani."

"I don't plan to. I'll go to the diner like always where there's always someone around. Gary's desperate. He'll make a mistake. Just like last night. He could have waited until I walked outside to grab me, but he was right at the door where I'd see him."

Luke poured some of his homemade granola into a bowl, added milk and a handful of blueberries, and slid it across the table to me. "He probably didn't expect you to have such a quick reaction. So, maybe you're right. Maybe he doesn't have a solid plan."

It made me feel better that Luke agreed with me.

"So, how will you lure him in?"

"You know why I slept well last night? I figured out a plan." I sampled the granola, crunchy and delicious.

"I'm all ears, Dani."

"Well, Gary will keep an eye on me, maybe from a distance, but he'll be around. When I go to my car, he'll make his move. He knows he can't just steal the ticket since I have that note from Thorne giving it to me. So, he'll have to force me to sign something, turning the ticket over to him, right? What do you think?"

Luke nodded. "I think he won't get close enough to do anything because I'm sticking with you today. AJ told me he wanted to grill Gary about last night but as far as I know, they're still looking for him. So, at the least, if he comes looking for you before they manage to nab him, AJ will bring him in for questioning. Sounds like a workable plan, Dani."

Pip had been patient while we talked and ate, but now she was antsy for her morning walk.

"A quick walk, then off to the diner?"

Luke took my hand and the three of us took our beach walk.

Would the plan work?

Chapter Thirty

WHEN LUKE AND I walked into the diner, Rose rushed to meet us. "AJ's waiting in that booth, Dani. He needs to talk to you."

"Give me a minute to check in with Chad."

"He's all set. I came in early to help make the scones and muffins. We have everything under control."

A customer signaled for a coffee refill, and she hustled away before I could argue, not that there was anything to argue about. Apparently, the Little Dog Diner didn't need me around. Sensations both welcome and uncomfortable churned in my gut, but I'd explore those feelings another time.

Luke, with Pip in his arms said, "I'll bring the Pipster to your office and give her some breakfast. Go talk to AJ. Fill him in on your plan."

What choice did I have? None, really, so I slid into the booth opposite AJ. He had coffee and the remnants of what looked like a chocolate chip muffin.

"Hey, Dani. I was about to give up on you showing

your face here." He raised his brows, hoping for an explanation.

I grinned. "Why would I do that, AJ?"

"Oh, I don't know. Maybe you're up to something you don't want me to know about?"

I shook my head. "Not after last night. That really shook me up. I need as many friendly people around me as possible."

"Good. I'm glad you've come to your senses. There's a murderer out there who wants something they think you have. You can't be too careful."

"Did you find Gary finally?

He looked away, never a good sign. "That's why I'm here, Dani. No, I didn't, but Detective Winter talked to his neighbor."

"Trudy?"

"You know her?" he said, surprised.

Luke brought me a mug of hot chocolate. The rich and creamy drink was just how I loved it, and I sipped it while I sorted out the conversation I'd had with Trudy.

"I don't know her well, but she comes in occasionally. I bumped into her yesterday. She's super friendly and chatty, kind of lonely I'm guessing. Anyway, while we were talking, she told me she was Thorne's neighbor. She met Gary and doesn't think much of him."

AJ moistened his finger and dabbed up the crumbs on his plate. "Yeah, that's the impression Detective

Winter got, too. The thing is, Trudy told Jane that she saw Gary load up his car late yesterday afternoon and drive away. We think he skipped town."

That didn't make sense. "He must have come back because he scared me half to death last night."

AJ's expression indicated pity, but did it mean he didn't believe me or was worried about me or both?

"Stay here today, Dani. We'll keep an eye on the diner in case he returns."

I decided to lay all my plans on the table. "I asked Luna to call Gary today and tell him she'll pay him to keep quiet about Bones's seizure disorder. That I'm cashing in the lottery ticket and using the money to buy her business. He doesn't know I gave it to you to keep safe."

AJ scowled. "Why would you do that, Dani? You're putting a target on your back."

"Listen, AJ. Thorne was killed because of that lottery ticket, and he entrusted it with me. If this flushes out the killer, it will put an end to this curse."

He pursed his lips. I could tell he was contemplating my plan, but would he go along with it? Finally, he said, "I'll have Detective Winter keep an eye on Luna's place in case Gary goes there. Who really knows what he'll do? I'll stick around here and watch over you, Dani. No ifs, ands, or buts about it, either."

That worked for me. I didn't want to take any risks

either.

Just as I finished my hot chocolate, we were all caught by surprise when Gary barged into the diner, eyes blazing, and strutting like a rooster ready for battle.

"Where is she? Where's my ticket?" he demanded as he scanned the diner. Finally landing his search on me.

Before he'd made a step in my direction though, AJ practically flew out of the booth. But Luke charged across the diner and beat him to Gary.

"Don't even think about doing anything," Luke said in a menacing tone I'd never heard before.

AJ quickly pushed between Luke and Gary, grabbing Gary's arm and pulling him toward the door. "You're coming with me. This has gone on long enough."

"You've got that right!" he said. "It's about time you people came to your senses and are ready to straighten out this mess. Thorne would want me to have the lottery ticket, not someone he barely even knew. Do you have it at the police station?"

AJ glanced at me. "We'll talk about it there, Gary. Let's go," he said, and they walked out.

Luke slid into the booth next to me, and Rose sat across from us.

"What the heck just happened? Is AJ giving the ticket to Gary?" Rose asked.

I laughed. "No way. All I can figure is that Gary jumped to a majorly wrong interpretation about what's going on and he sees it all in his favor. He's like that. At any rate, I can breathe now that AJ has him under control. It went a lot easier than I ever could have imagined."

"Yeah, I'm still processing it," Luke said. "I was ready to drag him outside and teach him a lesson. I'm glad it didn't come to that."

I squeezed Luke's hand. "Me, too."

Rose patted my hand and stood up. "It's busy this morning. Unfortunately, I can't sit here all day and chat with you."

"It's my diner. I'll get to work, too." I tried to push past Luke, but Rose held her hand up. "Nope. You stay here and relax, Dani. We'll call you the supervisor today." She laughed and walked to the kitchen.

"Rose is worried about you. You'd better do as she says," Luke said. "Mind if I run to Blueberry Acres? I want to check on my dad. I haven't seen him for a few days."

I waved him off with a flick of my wrist. "Absolutely. I'll sit right here while the customers enjoy their food. It's perfectly peaceful."

After kissing my cheek, Luke sauntered out.

I texted Sue Ellen and let her know that AJ had hauled Gary to the police station. I was sure Luna would sigh with relief after hearing that news. I mentally relaxed every one of my body parts, starting with my toes and working up to my neck, surprised at the amount of tension I'd been holding.

My phone beeped with a message—a thumbs-up from Sue Ellen.

Then, I got a new message from Kelly at Creative Design across the street. *"Dani, can you pop over for a sec? I have a question about AJ and Maggie's engagement."*

"Sure."

I jotted a quick message on a napkin to Rose that I'd be right back and scooted out. I jogged across the street and opened the door. It jingled with a welcoming sound as I walked inside.

Kelly was busy arranging beaded necklaces on a display.

"Exciting news about Maggie and AJ, isn't it?" I said.

She turned around and a big smile spread across her face. "I never thought that thickheaded brother of mine would ever pop the question." She laughed. "But now that he did, I want to plan an engagement party. Can you help?"

"Absolutely. How about at Sea Breeze?"

"I was hoping you'd say that."

I picked up one of the necklaces. "Pretty. It looks like one that Lyndsey had." It was still in my pocket, so I showed it to Kelly.

"That's the prototype, the one she kept for herself. When I saw it, I begged her to make more so she made all of these. They fly out of the store. As a matter of fact, I'm giving her a second chance to work here. I asked her to make more for me, but she said only if I gave her the job back." Kelly shrugged. "She's really good with the customers, and I'm keeping my fingers crossed that she'll be more reliable this time around. It will definitely be her last chance."

I thought Kelly was being very generous. "She's young and has a lot to learn. Good luck."

"Thanks. I have to get more inventory from the back. We'll talk more about the party another time, okay?"

"Looking forward to it."

Kelly walked into the back room, and I headed toward the door, already thinking about what I'd make for the engagement party.

The door opened just as I was reaching for the knob, so I stepped to the side to let the customer come in.

A person wearing a dark hoodie stood in front of me. I froze. Everything fell into place—the necklace, the sweatshirt, even the sunflower seed shells. Instantly, I realized how easy they were to plant. So many lies pointed to one person. There was no way she could pull off getting the ticket from me, though. Not here, not in the middle of town, with people around.

Lyndsey pulled the hood off her head and grabbed my arm. "Let's go," she said, her voice colder than ice water.

The necklace, her prototype, slipped through my fingers.

"You got away last night, but you won't be so lucky today. I have something you want, and I'm willing to make a trade."

I had no idea what she had that I'd want from her, but she grinned like her plan was foolproof. She pulled me outside and down the sidewalk to an alley.

Once we were out of everyone's sight, she sneered. "It just so happens that your little dog was waiting to cross the street, looking for you, I suppose. She wasn't happy when I grabbed her and shoved her in my car, but we couldn't have your little cutie get run over, could we? Now she's safe and sound on a quiet street where no one will hear her barking."

My legs went weak. It felt like all the blood drained from my face. I'd do anything to get Pip back, and Lyndsey knew it.

"Just a quick hike to Thorne's apartment where I parked my car. Neighbors are used to seeing it there, so it won't throw up any red flags. Then, you'll give me that lottery ticket along with a letter saying you've decided to turn it over to me, Lyndsey Malden. Sound good?" she said like she'd just offered to make me a cup of tea.

Lyndsey's fingers dug into my arm, but I walked as slowly as possible. Pip might not be happy, but she was safe, and the more time it took us to get to Lyndsey's car, the more time for someone to get to work finding me.

We stepped onto the sidewalk of a quiet street. No traffic, no kids playing outside, no one in their garden. When I saw Pip standing with her front paws on the dash of a small sedan, I almost shouted with joy. She was waiting and ready for action.

Now what?

"I don't have the ticket with me, Lyndsey."

"No problem. I'll drive you wherever we need to go. But don't try anything funny, or you'll never see that handsome husband of yours. I killed Thorne when he refused to give me the lottery ticket, and it's no skin off my back to kill again. Besides, everyone thinks Gary is the killer, and I've already left a trail of sunflower seeds pointing straight to him when you disappear."

I jerked, trying to pull away.

Lyndsey snarled. "It's you or the dog. What will it be?"

I stopped struggling.

Lyndsey looked up and down the street, then pulled me to the other side.

"Okay. You've thought of everything. The ticket is in my car at the Little Dog Diner."

"I don't believe you."

"It is. I was on my way to cash it in right after I left Creative Design." I held my breath that she believed this lie. Once we got to my car, I'd figure out some way to stall her.

Lyndsey scowled. "No wonder I couldn't find it at your friend's house. I was sure you'd given it to that detective for safekeeping. Okay, we'll go to your car, and if you want your dog back, you'll give me the ticket."

I nodded. What else could I do?

Pip barked and dug furiously on the dashboard, frantic to get out, but Lyndsey only laughed. What she didn't notice though, was Trudy peeking out from behind her curtain. She gave me a thumbs-up. I wasn't sure what it meant, but I hoped she grasped the situation clearly.

I quickly turned away from the apartment, hoping Lyndsey hadn't seen Trudy. "Let's get this over and done with. I want you out of my life," I said.

Lyndsey grinned. "Finally. You understand what you're up against."

I did, but did Lyndsey?

We retraced our steps. She stopped when we got back to Main Street and glanced both ways. "It looks nice and peaceful, just the way I like it. Let's go."

As soon as we were in front of Creative Design, ready to cross over to my car, AJ charged out of the store, grabbed Lyndsey, and pulled her away from me.

She screamed and fought like a tiger but never had a chance.

I backed away, not quite sure where to go, but suddenly Kelly was next to me with Rose and Sue Ellen right behind her. Everyone was yelling, I didn't know where to look until I saw Luke screech to a stop, causing the few other cars on Main Street to slam on their brakes, too.

I couldn't take my eyes off of Luke, my rock, my life.

Everyone asked at the same time, "Are you okay, Dani?"

"Yes, but I have to get Pip. She's in Lyndsey's car." I tried to run back to the alley.

"No, she's not." Trudy hustled over with my precious Pipster in her arms. "I got her as soon as you and that evil Lyndsey were out of sight. When she parked there, I couldn't figure out why your pup was inside. And when you two walked over, I assumed Lyndsey found Pip and you were coming to get her, but then you turned around and walked away. Something smelled rotten, so I called 911."

I hugged Trudy, crushing Pip between us. "Thank you. I had a plan, but yours was better."

Pip yipped and licked my chin. "You helped save the day, Pipster," I said as tears of happiness filled my eyes. "You let Trudy know I needed help."

AJ shoved Lyndsey into the back of a police cruiser then walked over to me. "Gary had an alibi for last night, so we had to let him go, but I told him if he came within a mile of you, I'd throw him in a cell. I'd recommend cashing in that ticket before you get yourself into any more trouble, Dani."

"That was always my plan, AJ, as soon as you give it back to me. I just had to be sure we scooped up the scandal and caught the killer first. Now, Luna can get on with her business of training black Labradors to help people in need."

Maggie climbed out of Luna's van along with Bones and Watson. "We just had our first lesson, Dani. Watch this," she said, apparently unaware of my close call with Lyndsey.

That was okay. I was thrilled Maggie found a healthy obsession. I wasn't sure if she'd saved Bones and Watson, or if it was other way around because in the end, it didn't really matter.

She stood still. The two black Labradors stared at her, and she said, "Sit." They both plopped their butts down and waited until Maggie gave them a treat.

Pip wiggled until I reluctantly put her down. She ran over and wiggled between the two dogs looking as cute as could be.

"Okay. You get a treat, too," Maggie said.

Luke put his arm around my shoulders and I nestled into his comforting embrace. When I looked at him, he nodded toward AJ who smiled with his eyes glued to Maggie. "They're perfect together, aren't they?"

I couldn't agree more.

The End

About the Author

Emmie Lyn grew up in a small town in New England, much like the towns where her female characters live—scenic, quaint and filled with colorful characters. She loves to create mysteries with twists and unexpected turns that draw readers in and capture their imagination.

Emmie lives in rural Massachusetts with her husband and a black cat with an extremely bad attitude. She shares twelve acres with a wide variety of wildlife including deer, bunnies, turkeys, and many songbirds. When she's not busy thinking of ways to kill off a character (for a book, of course!) she enjoys a cup of tea and chocolate in her flower garden, hiking, or spending time near the ocean.